BLADES OF HAVOC *book four*

death DROP

EVA CHANCE & HARLOW KING

Death Drop

Book 4 in the Blades of Havoc series

First Digital Edition, 2023

Cover design: The Pretty Little Design Co.

Ebook ISBN: 978-1-998752-41-6

Paperback ISBN: 978-1-998752-40-9

ONE

Luciana

WHEN THE NURSE came into the hospital waiting room again, I felt as if I'd been sitting on the edge of my seat for hours. Jasper automatically grasped my hand as the woman motioned for us to get up. She only spoke broken English, but Niko's sister, Emi, had explained to her in Japanese that we'd want to visit after she and Niko's parents had seen the patient.

I scrambled to my feet and followed the nurse, my heart thudding against my ribs in a strange mix of relief and fear. Yesterday had been the worst day of my life: watching Niko's limp body loaded into an ambulance, failing to get anyone to tell me whether he had a chance of surviving. Pacing this waiting room until visiting hours were over, only getting sporadic updates from Emi, who'd looked equally horrified.

He'd been in surgery and knocked out on medication, but late this morning he'd finally come to. Naturally his family had wanted to spend time with him first. I couldn't resent them, as anxious as I was to see with my own eyes that he was okay.

Or at least as close to okay as you could get after taking a couple of bullets in the chest.

Jasper stuck close by my side as we strode down the hall, his gray-green eyes clouded with his own worries. His tall presence would have felt more reassuring if his broad shoulders hadn't been rigid with tension.

A police officer stood outside Niko's door, in consideration of the fact that his injuries had been due to an awful crime by assailants who hadn't been arrested yet. I knew that Rafael was monitoring the hospital on the outside, watching for anyone suspicious, but my stomach stayed knotted.

Would my mother's thugs make another attempt at Niko's life? Or at mine and my other lovers'?

Quentin had opted to help Rafael with his external surveillance, figuring Niko wouldn't want to see him all that urgently. But he'd given me a tight hug before I'd come inside this morning. "He'll come through. He might not look so tough, but that guy is made of strong stuff."

I couldn't have been more glad that he'd been proven right.

As we came up on the room, Emi emerged, ushering out a middle-aged couple while she chattered away in low but rapid Japanese. She shot me a glance over her shoulder with a swish of her sleek black bob and winked before guiding her parents in the opposite direction down the hall.

Emi and I had become fast friends when she'd come to visit Niko in Boston and eagerly cheered me and Jasper on in our qualifying competition. She'd realized I was dating not just her older brother but my skating partner and my bodyguard as well and accepted the unusual relationship without blinking.

But during our first get-together after we'd arrived in Tokyo to train for the World Championships, which were happening next month in Nagano, she'd told me that we were better off not trying to explain things to their parents. "The older generation," she said with a tsk of her tongue as if that explained everything. "They struggle enough with the idea that Niko likes girls *and* boys without him dating both at the same time."

Which he was doing. Jasper was as much Niko's lover as I was, even if they hadn't taken their physical relationship to quite the same level just yet. Considering that when I'd first met them, neither of them had been willing to even admit their feelings for each other, they'd come a long way.

The nurse motioned for us to stop just outside the room. As she slipped inside to confirm that Niko was ready to see us, the police officer gave us an inscrutable onceover. I hoped he was taking his job seriously.

Of course, *I* was the one who'd really failed here. It'd been my mother's goons who'd attacked us and shot Niko. Somewhere along the line, I hadn't been careful enough in covering my tracks.

Or maybe it went all the way back to my selfish desire

to pursue my skating dreams. I'd known how angry Mom was about my decision to leave Austin. She'd threatened my men multiple times in the past.

I should have realized there was no way they'd be safe as long as they were with me.

The nurse returned and bobbed her head to us. "You may go now," she said in her halting English.

Jasper swiped his hand through his shaggy auburn locks and set his jaw before stepping inside. I hurried after him, my pulse thumping even faster.

At the sight that met me beyond the door, my heart just about leapt right out of my chest. Niko was sitting up in the hospital bed, propped against a couple of pillows. His warm smile somehow shone as bright as always, but I could see the strain in the rest of his face. And there was no ignoring the bandages bulging beneath his hospital gown or the IV hooked up to his wrist.

Jasper went straight to him and grasped his free hand. "How are you doing? No, that's a stupid question. I'm so glad you pulled through. Is there anything we can get for you?"

Niko let out a laugh that was only slightly raspy. "Who knew all it'd take to make you more talkative was me getting shot?"

I grimaced as I came up at our coach's other side, but my mouth sprang back into a joyful smile a second later. "It's just so good to see you awake and doing better. We were so worried. Jasper's right—if you need anything at all—"

Niko held up his hand, still clasped in Jasper's larger one, and his bright brown eyes twinkled with amusement.

"I think the hospital staff has that covered. Not that I mind your kindness."

Jasper swallowed audibly. "Have the doctors said anything about your recovery? Or how long they'll need to monitor you for?"

Niko shook his head, the neon pink streak dyed into the smooth black strands swaying with movement. "They're running a few more tests. But it seems hopeful. Unless something unexpected appears, it sounds like I should be back on my feet in a day or two. Just… moving slowly for a little while after that."

"Of course." My throat closed up for a moment before I could force the words out. "I'm so sorry, Niko. It was all my fault. If I hadn't turned against my mom—"

Niko shook his head again, vehemently enough that my voice died. "Don't say that. I made my own choices—and I'm happy with them. I know the risks, and I still think they were worth it to see you and Jasper shine."

Jasper's mouth twisted. "Niko… You almost *died*."

Our coach shot him a firm look. "But I didn't die. We showed those gangsters we won't be stopped that easily. From now on, we'll just have to be even more careful."

My jaw dropped with a lurch of my gut. "From now on? You want us to keep training?"

Niko chuckled. "Of course I do. The world needs your talent. This was only a minor obstacle along the way to your glory."

"I'd hardly call this minor," I sputtered with a frantic wave toward his hospital bed.

"In a few weeks, it'll only be a memory," Niko insisted.

"You have a… a gift. I'm not letting anyone scare you away from sharing it."

Jasper's voice went rough. "You shouldn't even be thinking about that right now. Not when we almost lost you completely."

Niko gazed up at him, his expression softening. "I'm still here."

My partner's Adam's apple bobbed. He blinked hard, a sheen of unshed tears coming into his stormy eyes. A flush crept up his neck to his cheeks, and he seemed to stumble over his next words. "And thank God for that. I—I'll get you something to drink."

He leaned in to give Niko a quick but tender kiss and then hustled for the door. As I glanced after him, I thought I saw him start to swipe at his eyes just before he disappeared from view.

I'd never seen Jasper get that emotional before. The poor guy didn't know how to cope.

But then, could I blame him? I hardly knew how to hold *myself* together after the trauma we'd just been through. Niko had gotten by far the worst of it—how could he still be so chipper?

When I turned back to our coach, his smile had deflated. His gaze lingered on the doorway after Jasper had left. I wished my partner could have seen how much our mutual boyfriend would rather have had him here, emotional or not.

Then Niko's attention shifted back to me. He reached across his chest to grasp my forearm. "Don't look so sad, Angel. It's over now."

I lowered my gaze. "But is it? We don't know when my

mom might send more people. We don't even know for sure that you're totally okay now."

"We'll—how do you say it—cross that bridge when we get there? You've found ways to deal with her before." He paused and gave my arm a squeeze. "Enough about that. I need to tell you something."

I met his gaze, an ache spreading through my chest. "What?"

His smile returned, delicate but brilliant all the same. "I love you, Lou. I don't want to wait any longer to tell you that and risk losing the chance. And I'd get shot with a hundred more bullets just to watch you skate a few more times. So you're not allowed to stop because of this or to feel guilty about it."

My own tears blurred my vision. I set my hand over his, gripping his fingers tightly. "I don't think I can help the guilt. But I love you too, Niko. So much. That's why I'm so scared."

He lifted his hand higher to stroke his fingers over my cheek. "You're meant to be on the ice. And I think I'm meant to help you become everything you're capable of. It's simply destiny. You can't argue with that."

A laugh hitched out of me. I leaned in and gave him as much of a hug as I could without hurting him more. Niko tipped his head forward to brush his lips against my hair.

I eased up so I could claim a proper kiss, if a brief one. Then I met his eyes with all the conviction I had in me. "If it matters that much to you, I'll keep going. For me and for you. But I'm also going to do everything in my power to make sure my mom can't hurt anyone else."

Even saying that sent a chill down my spine. How much power did I have compared to Mom's empire?

But I had allies. I had the advantage none of her greater enemies had of knowing her well. If there was a way to stop her reign of terror for good, I'd find it.

Niko's face glowed with affection. "You wouldn't be my angel if you'd say anything else."

The door squeaked open again. I glanced over, expecting Jasper to have returned, but the nurse poked her head inside. She murmured something to Niko in Japanese.

He nodded to her and gave me a regretful look. "She says visiting time is over. They don't want me to push myself too hard when I've just woken up."

I choked up automatically and did my best to hide it. "I wouldn't want to wear you out when you need to be healing either. We'll be back as soon as we can."

He trailed his fingertips over my arm as I stepped away. "I'll be looking forward to it. And Lou, could you do one thing for me?"

I stopped. "Anything you want."

His smile turned crooked. "It's nothing big. I'm counting on them giving me a little more family time. Tell Emi that there's one more thing I need to talk to her about."

TWO

Luciana

I HAD no inkling what Niko might have been up to until Emi texted me the next morning to announce that she was picking up me and the guys—to bring us to our new rink.

"You'll like this place," she chirped as I got into the passenger seat of her compact Honda while Quentin and Jasper slid into the back. "They look after it really nice, and it's got some of the best security you'll find for an arena in Tokyo."

I glanced over my shoulder toward Rafael, newly cast-free, who was insisting on tailing us in the rental SUV Niko had arranged for us when we first arrived in the country. "How secure is that?"

Emi laughed and eased the car into the flow of traffic outside our apartment building. "Let's just say this is where a bunch of rich kids go to practice — and when I say rich, I'm talking about the kind of kids who think money will buy them a way into a fancy skating career. They're wrong, of course, but their parents don't want anything happening to them while they're pretending to be professionals."

"Rich, huh?" Jasper said doubtfully. "How much is the ice time going to set us back?"

"Nothing!" Emi shot him a grin in the rearview mirror. "I set things up through the owner's niece, who's a friend. I promised her uncle that if you two win a medal at the World Championships, he can tell everyone you practiced on his rink. It'll be the first time anyone who trained there even made it to a big competition. Might be a chance for him to get taken more seriously."

I guessed that was a reasonable trade-off. I didn't love the idea of hanging out some place funded by the city's elite, giving the trappings of quality even though apparently they weren't turning out any top skaters. But if no one prominent had ever come out of there, then the place wouldn't be on anyone's radar when looking for Worlds-level competitors.

And rich-people-level security sounded good to me. I'd do just about anything to avoid a repeat of our last practice's bloodshed.

As if he were thinking along similar lines, Quentin shook his head. "I can't believe Okabe was worrying about finding you a new practice space before he's even out of the hospital. That guy's a maniac."

"Only in the best way," Emi said cheerfully. "He's always been obsessed with skating. And now he has two other people to obsess over instead of just his own performance."

Jasper let out a rough guffaw.

I peered through the windows at the shiny skyscrapers we were gradually leaving behind. If I'd learned anything in the short time I'd been living in Tokyo, it was that any time I thought I understood how huge the city was, it got even bigger. It didn't have one downtown but something like a dozen of them.

Austin looked like some podunk town next to this metropolis.

Emi wove through the streets with total confidence, bringing us into a neighborhood of low-rise buildings in a hotchpotch of grays, beiges, and browns. She rounded the corner and drew into a small parking lot outside a silvery domed building. A red sign out front held thick Japanese characters next to smaller print in English that said SPORTS GARDEN.

Rafael parked next to us and got out, his dark eyes scanning the lot. I suspected the low but sturdy wall that surrounded the place garnered a little approval.

As we walked up to the front doors, Emi produced three key cards from her purse. "I got one for each of you skaters, and I have one for Niko too, after he's on his feet again. No regular keys, so no one can make copies. And there's always someone on watch at the security desk."

She gave the stern-looking man behind the desk in the lobby a friendly wave. He dipped his head slightly to us, his gaze sliding right back toward the parking lot.

Well, that was definitely a step up from rinks so low-key there was rarely anyone watching the reception area at all.

Emi led us through a couple of sparkling clean hallways and pointed out the locker rooms. "It looks like you're already in your practice clothing, though, so we can go right in to the rink. You've got the next three hours, but we can book longer sessions on the weekdays when most of the usual trainees are in school until the late afternoon."

She pushed past another set of double doors, and a waft of chilly air swept over me. My nerves settled a little at the familiar calm of the vast, quiet room. My hand dropped to my equipment bag, the urge gripping me to pull on my skates and vanish completely into the escape skating could bring as quickly as possible.

Emi gave me a knowing look. "You can get started. I have to meet with my parents. If you need anything, give me a call."

I nodded. "We'll see you at the hospital in the afternoon, if our paths cross."

She smiled back at me. "And not too long after that even if they don't. Have fun!"

As she slipped out, my men and I tramped past the stands to the rink itself. Rafael hunkered down on a bench about halfway between the door and the ice, turning so he could keep an eye on both at once.

I dropped onto another bench and groped in my bag for my skates and my gloves. The sooner I was on the ice, the better.

I tied the final knot, shucked off the skate guards, and stepped onto the rink. The first glide forward sent a wave of peace rushing through me.

Moments later, Jasper joined me. We automatically fell into the paces of our typical warm-up routine, stretching and getting our heartrate going, sweeping back and forth across the ice.

"Let's do some individual jumps and spins so we're totally used to the space before we get into anything more complicated," Jasper suggested when we'd finished.

Quentin appeared to be already doing that, whipping around at the far end of the rink, favoring his mostly-healed shoulder only a little now. I swiped my gloved hands together. "Sure, that sounds like a good idea. Double axels?"

My partner flashed me a smile. "You called it."

We took turns picking our next move, the hiss of our skates against the frozen surface providing the only soundtrack.

Too quiet a soundtrack. The sound was soothing, yes, but it wasn't enough. I couldn't stop myself from listening for Niko's voice calling out encouragement and advice.

None of this was the same without our coach here. How could we focus when the horror that'd taken him down was lingering in the back of all our minds?

If it hadn't been for Niko, Jasper and I would never have given this partnership a thought. He'd brought us together and bound us with his warm enthusiasm, which had proven to be unshakable even in the face of multiple gunshot wounds.

Maybe someday I'd be able to imagine doing this without him, but not any time soon.

Jasper paused when we eased apart after a joint spin, taking in my expression. "Are you okay?"

My mouth twisted. "Just… missing Niko."

A shadow crossed his face. "Yeah. Me too. I skated for all those years before I even met him, but now… it's like he's an essential part of this whole experience."

"He really is."

I dragged in a breath and was going to say that we should try with music, because that's what Niko would have suggested. A peal of a much more electronic-sounding tone than I'd had in mind cut me off.

"My phone." I pushed off toward the stands to check it. Maybe it was Emi with more news—or Niko himself, reaching out from the hospital.

What if something more had happened to him? Could Mom's goons have gotten past the police presence there?

My heart was thumping hard by the time I snatched up my phone. I stared at the text on the screen, my fear shifting from one source to another in an instant.

"Who is it?" Rafael asked, shoving himself to his feet.

"I… I don't know. Someone who knows who I am. But I have no idea how they got this number."

Hello, Miss Cordova, the text message read. *We've come to Tokyo to support you as the true heir to the Deadly Rose. I think we could have something to offer you. Will you meet up with us?*

Jasper had clomped over and checked the text over my shoulder. "What the hell? Is this some kind of joke?"

"I don't think so," I said slowly. "Why would anyone joke about that? No one who isn't part of my old life would know to mention 'Deadly Rose' or my real last name."

Rafael scanned the words with a deepening frown. "They want you to meet them? It sounds like a trap."

"It could be." Tension wrapped around my gut. "But I can't just ignore this, can I? If I don't answer, and they're out to hurt me, they'll force the issue. This way, we might be able to scope them out before we have to deal with them directly."

Quentin had joined us. When I held out the phone to show him the message too, he cocked his head. "We might as well find out what they want, right? You had other people from that Devil's Dozen group help you. Maybe they actually are on your side."

I rubbed my mouth. "Possible, but not super likely. But I'd rather find out what I'm up against than stay in the dark." It'd be better to confront them now than to wait and see if they burst into this rink with another hail of gunfire.

I typed out a hasty reply. *Who are you? And what are you offering?*

The answer came immediately. *I think that'd be easier to discuss in person. We'd rather not risk your phone being tapped and the conversation overheard. If Mireya hears about this, it'll go much worse for us than for you.*

Okay, I guessed that was a fair point, if they were planning to stand with me against her. I worried at my lower lip. *Fine. Where can I find you?*

Shinjuku Gyoen. We can get there in ten minutes. We'll wait near the bridge past the Rakuu-Tei tea house for an hour.

Rafael was already typing on his phone. "We can get

to the park in half an hour. That'll give us a little time to study them before we decide whether to hear them out."

I lowered my phone to my side, my fingers clutching it tightly. "All right. Let's see who's come out to play."

Rafael found a parking space a few streets over from the park, which looked huge on my phone's map. The map did show the tea house the text had mentioned, with a pond and a couple of bridges nearby, so at least we had some idea where we were going.

The early February breeze had a nip to it but nothing outright biting. Niko had told us that it did snow in Tokyo, but only rarely. We headed into the park, where many of the trees had kept their greenery, although skeletal leafless branches showed in patches here and there.

Only a few visitors strolled beneath the trees. I hadn't visited this park before, and the serenity of it seeped into my skin despite my jangling nerves. I'd have liked to see it in the full bloom of springtime.

As we came up on the tea house, regularly consulting our phone maps, we slowed. Most of the bystanders were obviously Japanese locals, who paid us no attention. I saw two pairs I easily identified as tourists from the way they were holding up their phones and tapping away at the camera buttons. No one appeared to be looking for us yet.

Rafael peered at the map and motioned to the path ahead of us. "It looks like the trees thin up ahead and there's a pretty large clearing past the tea house, near the pond. If they're waiting there, we'll be able to get a good look at them without them seeing us yet. Keep your eyes peeled."

As we followed him off the path through one last dense stretch of trees, his hand rested on his hip. He had a pistol concealed there, under his leather jacket.

Just ahead of us, the trees gave way to a span of clear lawn. We slunk through the shadows to the edge of where we could stay concealed and peered out over the garden.

It was a pretty spectacular view. Maybe a hundred feet away lay a tranquil pond, rippling faintly with the breeze. An immense skyscraper and several other high rises showed over the tops of the trees that ringed the far side of the water, reminding us that this apparent wilderness lay in the middle of a vast modern city.

Then three figures ambled into view on the grass between our vantage point and the pond-side path.

I knew at once that they were the ones who'd sent that message. None of them were Japanese, but they didn't have the attitude of tourists either. They stuck close together, their eyes scanning the scenery as if they were as nervous of us as we were of them.

As I squinted at them, recognition crept over me. The big Latino guy with the lightning bolt shaved into his buzzcut—I'd seen him around the Deadly Rose mansion back in Austin. The woman too—her straggly bleached-blond waves and sharply arched eyebrows would have made her easy to pick out of a crowd even if female underlings hadn't been relatively rare.

The third guy, tall and scrawny with a thick scar that cut across his cheek just below his right eye, I'd never seen before. But if he was in with the other two, he'd definitely worked for my mom.

I glanced at Rafael, who was still contemplating them. "They were all part of the Austin outfit," he confirmed in a low voice. "In the middle of the ranks, not much authority but not newbies either. I never had much to do with any of them, though."

"They're *here*, like they said they'd be," Quentin pointed out. "It doesn't look like they brought any backup. We've already got them outnumbered."

I wet my lips. I could probably take at least one of them on my own, and Rafael definitely could. And we hadn't seen any sign of an ambush as we'd snuck over here.

If anything, the trio had put themselves in a weaker position, out there in the open with no shelter nearby. We could have shot them all down in a matter of seconds if we'd wanted to.

"You really want to do this?" Jasper asked me.

I shrugged. "We came all this way. They might have useful information."

Rafael sighed. "All right. But call them over here. I don't want *us* out in the open for this conversation either."

Bracing myself in case I needed to run or hit the ground, I stepped from between the trees at the edge of the lawn. "Hey! Waiting for me?"

The trio jerked around, the woman's face brightening in relief and the two men both looking vaguely grouchy but also awkward about it. I wheeled my arm, motioning for them to join us in the shelter of the trees.

As they stalked over, a tight smile curled the woman's

lips. "You came. I'm glad to see I wasn't wrong that you've got plenty of guts."

Rafael flanked me, his gun in his hand now. "She's got more than that. You'd better start explaining what you're up to *now*, or we're out of here."

"Yeah," Quentin added. "You said you've got something to offer Lou. What is it?"

The big guy with the buzzcut gave Rafael a thoughtful look as if evaluating who would win in a fight—and seemed to deflate a bit when he must have decided it wouldn't be him.

His skinnier companion cleared his throat, spat on the ground, and gave us a crooked smile of his own. "Honestly, it's actually more about what we hope you can do for us."

"But we can help you too," the woman insisted.

I folded my arms over my chest. "What are you talking about? Let's get to the actual explanation faster, please."

The scrawny man narrowed his eyes, making the scar rise on his cheek. "You've seen how your mother has gotten. Going off the rails, lashing out at people—half the time when they haven't even done anything wrong. We figure we're better off not following her orders than trying to stay in line."

Mr. Lightning Buzzcut nodded. "She can't keep up like this for long, not with the mess she's gotten into. You'll be the new Deadly Rose soon. So we came to you."

The woman sketched a faux curtsy. "We're here to prove our loyalty. Take us under your protection, and we'll let you know anything we find out about your mother's plans. We'll stand with you if she sends anyone after you."

I had to hold back a laugh. These three figured *I* could protect them? I hadn't even been able to keep my coach and lover safe. They might be better off pretending they'd never heard of the Cordova family at all.

But they were here. They were making an appeal to me. There could be safety in numbers for both of us.

And if I wanted to keep my men out of the worst danger from here forward, having whatever intel these defectors could pass on could make all the difference.

"I can't make any promises," I said, unwilling to lie. "It's not like I have the kind of manpower my mother can wield. But if you're willing to work for me, I'll do what I can to take care of you."

As soon as I was sure I could actually trust them. I considered my options. "Do you have a secure place to stay?"

Scarface wrinkled his nose. "We've been hiding out in one of the local hostels. Not exactly prime digs."

I hummed to myself. "That'll have a lot of people coming and going. We'll have to fix that. Our apartment at the Izumi Tower is already pretty crowded, but I'll see about getting you a place nearby where you can lay low as soon as possible."

The woman let out her breath in a rush. "That would be an amazing start."

I took out my phone. "Let me get your names and numbers so I can get in touch."

It turned out the woman was Ursula, the big buzzcut dude was Dámaso, and the scarred guy went by Frankie. I saved their numbers in my phone and lifted my head to meet Ursula's gaze again, since she seemed the most eager of the bunch.

"How exactly did you get *my* number?" Only a few people in the Deadly Rose ranks had gotten a direct line to the heir apparent, and the three lackeys in front of me weren't among that number.

The trio exchanged a glance. Ursula jabbed her thumb toward Frankie. "This guy managed to take a peek at Mireya's contacts and wrote it down. I told him he was insane, but I guess it worked out in our favor."

Frankie grinned. "Let's hope so."

We parted ways, the gangsters heading across one of the bridges and us backtracking the way we'd come. When we were well out of earshot, Jasper shot me a sideways glance. "What's the Izumi Tower? The place we're staying isn't called anything like that."

I smiled slyly in return. "I know. I noticed it during one of my grocery runs—it's a building a few blocks down the street." I turned to Rafael. "I'll need you to keep an eye on it for the next few days to see if my mother launches any attacks there. If she does, then we know our new friends were looking to double-cross us and passed the info back to her."

Rafael let out a low chuckle. "Smart thinking. I've made a couple of contacts on the wrong side of the tracks while you were off skating over the past couple of weeks… I can arrange to have the building watched."

I took a gulp of the crisp air and let it wash some of the tension from my lungs. "Well, our rink time would be over by now anyway. Let's head to the hospital. We can grab some lunch and eat with Niko if his parents are done visiting for the morning."

Quentin rubbed his hands together. "Sounds good to me."

It was a short trip from where Rafael had parked the car to the hospital where Niko had been admitted. I watched Rafael navigate the unfamiliar streets with a mix of affection and awe. He hadn't even been fully mobile for most of his time in this new country, still recovering from his own injuries after an attack by his brother's old gang back in Austin, but he'd managed to adapt in all kinds of ways already.

The hospital's underground lot was pretty full. We had to park a couple of rows over from the elevator. As we headed over through the artificial light, two men in well-fitted suits stepped into our path.

What now? I couldn't help thinking as I jerked to a halt, my body shifting into a defensive pose. Rafael's hand shot to his holster.

"You don't want to do that," one of the men said smoothly with a flick of his eyes toward the gun. "We're here on behalf of the Bright Dragon and the March Wind of the Devil's Dozen."

Oh, shit.

THREE

Luciana

FACING off against two representatives for the world's top criminal masterminds wasn't quite as scary as dealing with the head honchos themselves, but only by an increment. The thirteen crime bosses who made up the Devil's Dozen were the most powerful figures in existence, considering that between them they controlled all of the illegal activity around the globe except the pettiest of crimes that could escape their notice.

Mom was one of them. I'd met a couple who didn't seem all that bad. But the majority, to get where they were, had turned brutality into an artform. And the two men in front of us were no doubt sanctioned to act on their behalf.

I held myself still and steady, trying to keep a calm expression even as my pulse thundered through my veins.

These weren't the kind of people I'd want to show any weakness in front of. "All right. We're listening. What exactly do you want?"

The man on the left, a burly dude who looked Asian but not like most of the Japanese locals I'd met—maybe Chinese?—flicked a discreet gun from a holster under his suit jacket and held it lowered but in view. He spoke with a polished British accent. "The Bright Dragon would like to know what your presence in Tokyo means in terms of your mother's intentions."

The other guy, his jowled head topped by tufts of bright red hair, palmed a pistol of his own. He aimed both it and a glare at me, spitting out his words with a mild Australian drawl. "And the March Wind would like to hear what the fuck you were angling for, sending around all those files about her operations."

His tone was sharper than his companions, and his posture undeniably aggressive. I fought the urge to take a step back from him, seeing Rafael's fingers close around the grip of his gun.

Mom hadn't just made enemies with her plotting against her fellow Devil's Dozen members. She'd had at least a few allies who were scheming right alongside her to take down some of their colleagues and divide territory they stole between them. From this guy's demeanor, I couldn't help wondering if my gambit had upended the March Wind's plans as well as my mother's.

Otherwise you'd think he'd have appreciated the warning rather than sounding pissed off about it.

"I think the answer to the second question should cover both," I said tartly, as if I were annoyed by the interruption, not terrified for the men standing with me. "I disagreed with my mother's tactics, and I figured the rest of you should know that she was hoping to tear apart the foundations of your organization. I also wanted to get her off my back. I'm not interested in inheriting her spot at the table."

The March Wind's man made a scoffing sound. "And we're just supposed to believe that?"

I glared right back at him. "Yes. Because if you did even a fraction of the research I'm sure your boss would have expected, you'll have seen that I'm here to compete in the World Figure Skating Championships. Which are taking place in Nagano, so of course I'm in Japan. We're training in Tokyo to try to avoid having my mom's people track us down, although that hasn't worked out so well after all."

The Bright Dragon's man studied me with a cooler gaze. "And what is your game plan after this skating competition? Are you aiming to wrestle your mother's empire away from her?"

I couldn't stop myself from rolling my eyes. "Did you listen to anything I just said? She can keep her empire. I just don't want her having *me*. She was using threats to keep me under her thumb, so I exposed her so that she'd have bigger problems to deal with. I'd be happiest if she forgets I even exist and I can focus on nothing but skating and regular life."

"As if the heir to the Deadly Rose would ever give up all ambition," the March Wind's man sneered. "We know where you came from. It sounds like this is all another game to me, one you won't win."

I folded my arms over my chest. "The only thing I care about winning is medals on the ice. I haven't had any contact with the criminal world since I left Austin, other than whatever my bodyguard has needed to do to keep us safe. But maybe you're more concerned because of what your boss thought *he* was going to win if my mother got to see through her plans."

I knew the second the accusation flew from my lips that it'd been a miscalculation. The stutter of the man's expression gave away that I was right, but his eyes flashed an instant later, his gun hand jerking forward. "I don't need to listen to a snake like you talk about my employer that way. Unless you want to know what the inside of your skull looks like."

None of us were slow draws around here. Not after all of my boyfriends had gotten weeks of practice with their own weapons that Rafael had managed to smuggle over the ocean.

A second after the threatening gesture, I'd tugged my tiny pistol from my purse into my hand, and Jasper and Quentin had retrieved their weapons from their concealed positions as well. The March Wind's rep flicked his gaze over all of us, a bit of the color fading from his ruddy cheeks.

He'd figured at least some of my men wouldn't be prepared. He'd bet wrong.

"Let's simmer down," the Bright Wind's man said in an even tone. "You have to understand that it's difficult for any of us to believe you gave up all of that power simply to skate."

Rafael stepped forward, gun ready but not aimed, his

eyes glinting dangerously. "Is it really? Do *you* enjoy every part of this job? Lou's spent her whole life in a position where she has no more control over what she does and where she goes than you do. And she loves doing something her mother sees as silly. You've got to have enough imagination to see how all that supposed power could become a cage."

I'd rarely heard him speak at that much length, but his conviction rang through his words—and the March Wind's man lowered his gun just slightly at hearing it put that way. And maybe because it was coming from another man rather than a girl he probably saw as silly too.

My bodyguard had been part of criminal negotiations like this for nearly as long as I'd been alive. It made sense that he'd be comfortable talking at these men's level—and making the right points to start to diffuse their apprehension.

I raised my hand to rest it on the back of Rafael's elbow, surreptitiously encouraging him taking the initiative. "That's right. I don't feel powerful when I'm with my mother—I feel confined. And no amount of money holds a candle to the thrill of performing a routine that brings an audience to their feet with applause."

The March Wind's man scowled. "And with all those performances, you're risking bringing the Devil's Dozen into the public eye. There's already been too much talk on the news about the attack on your coach."

I sighed. "And who do you think orchestrated that attack? If you're upset about it, take it up with my mom. I'd rather it'd never happened in the first place."

Rafael nodded. "If anything, that should be more

proof to you that Luciana is completely at odds with the Deadly Rose. She was almost killed in that ambush. The goons her mother sent didn't hold their fire."

"Yeah." I lifted my chin. "So if you have a problem with the spotlight that's being pointed on those crimes, you should be focusing on the Deadly Rose, not me. If there are no more attacks on me and my friends, then I won't even *think* about the Devil's Dozen again."

"And if there are?" the Bright Dragon's rep asked. "Are you threatening to expose us?"

Oh, for fuck's sake. I held myself back from gritting my teeth. "No, I'm just pointing out the natural consequences of my mother's insanity. She's the one sending people to shoot at me. Believe me, if I could make her stop, I would."

Rafael raised an eyebrow. "And your bosses should know how difficult it is to stop the Deadly Rose, considering the conflict with the entire Devil's Dozen hasn't managed to stop her campaign of vengeance against her daughter for even a couple of weeks. Are they coming down on their colleague as hard as you're coming down on Lou?"

The burly man's mouth twisted with a hint of a grimace. The March Wind's man raked his hand back through his fiery hair.

"I'm telling you," I said, just to drive the point home, "I'm not part of the Deadly Rose's empire or her family anymore in any way that matters. Everything you could possibly dig up about my activities here in Tokyo or the months last year when I left Austin should confirm that.

My mother has all the control here. I'm just clinging to the little scrap of freedom I've been able to steal away."

There was a moment of tense silence. Then both of the men holstered their weapons.

"I'll pass on your remarks to my employer and see what he makes of them," the Bright Dragon's man said with a brief dip of his head.

The March Wind's rep let out a huff but nodded in a brusquer gesture than his companion's. "Yeah, yeah. We'll look into it. I don't think the boss will be happy about it though, so you'd better be ready to do some more explaining."

They split off from each other, moving quickly to their respective vehicles. I didn't take another full breath until the cars had rumbled, one after the other, out of the underground garage.

As the guys put away their own guns, my shoulders sagged. "Holy hell."

I tipped my face toward the dark ceiling. "No more surprises, okay, universe? I can't take another one."

FOUR

Rafael

LOU HAD ALWAYS BEEN good at putting on a tough front. It would have been one of the very first lessons she learned living under her mother's roof. But I knew her well enough to see the slight stiffness to her movements as she reached for the plates to clear the table after our dinner, to notice the way her smile faded too quickly when Quentin made a teasing remark.

I could understand why she'd be stressed. Not only did she have Niko to worry about, even if he'd been looking even better during our visit this afternoon, but now she was facing more intrusions and threats from our old life.

If it'd been up to me, I'd have sheltered her from everything except the parts of her life she loved. But I hadn't managed to fully protect her even when she'd only wanted to train with Coach Balakin back in Austin. Who would I be kidding if I tried to convince myself I could shield her from everything coming at us now?

I kept an eye on her as she rinsed the dishes, but I didn't push. When she was ready to talk through whatever was at the front of her mind, she would.

As I wiped off the compact apartment's small table, Quentin switched to hassling Jasper about some skating thing I couldn't give a shit about.

"I can't believe you'd put that Daimos routine in your top five. He didn't even manage to land the full triple Axel."

Jasper shot the younger guy a look that was more exasperated than outright angry. "Of course he did. I've watched that performance dozens of times."

Quentin shook his head. "No way. He pulled out a split-second too early. Anyone with eyes would have noticed that."

"The judges scored it like he completed the rotation."

"Right, and we all know that judges never make mistakes. Especially when they've got a world champion they're *supposed* to fawn over in front of them."

Jasper let out a huff and motioned for Quentin to follow him. "There's an easy way to settle this. I've got a video recording on my computer. We can even play it in slow motion if you insist."

"You'll be the one crying afterward."

Their voices dwindled as they stepped into Jasper's bedroom. Lou watched them go and rolled her eyes. "Boys."

I couldn't hold back a smirk. "Hey, you're the one who wanted them around."

"It's a good thing they have so many good points as well." She managed a wider grin and came over to grasp my hand. "But this means I can get a little one-on-one time with the only guy who won't argue about rotations or leg angles."

I laughed and let her guide me over to the sofa. Like the other furniture in the apartment Niko had arranged for us, it was smaller than I'd have preferred. I guessed there weren't a whole lot of Japanese men with quite my height and heft. But I could make do with the narrow cushions in exchange for a cuddle with my woman.

Lou tugged me down beside her and tucked her legs over my lap while resting her head on my chest. I slung my arm around her automatically. She sighed, relaxing into my embrace in a way that was as gratifying as making her moan between the sheets.

"Have you heard anything from the people who've been watching Izumi Tower?" she asked. "Any sign that my mother's people have poked around there?"

I stroked my thumb over the peak of her shoulder. "My main guy has only been in place for a few hours, but so far, nothing. I don't think we can draw any conclusions until we've given it at least a couple of days, though."

"Yeah." Her next sigh sounded tense again. "What do you think I should do about those three turncoats who came looking for me? Even if they don't tattle to my mom right away, that's no guarantee they won't later. And then there's the asshole reps from those two Devil's Dozen bigwigs… What if they're not satisfied with the answers I gave them?"

She was asking me? I hesitated, willing my muscles to

stay loose beneath her body so she couldn't feel me tensing up.

I guessed it made sense for her to want my opinion. I was the only one she could count on here who had any significant experience with that part of her life. It wasn't as if the skater guys could offer much insight into the criminal mindset.

I traced more soothing patterns on her arm as I contemplated my answer. "I think you started off on the right foot. You didn't give the defectors any real information and found a way to test their loyalties. And you pushed the Devil's Dozen pendejos to focus on your mother rather than you. That's definitely the direction their attention should be pointed in."

"It just seems like hardly anything."

"Hey." I eased her closer and pressed a kiss to her forehead. "Listen to me. You showed them you're no one to be messed with but made your stance clear at the same time. No one could have handled it better."

"I think you might be a bit biased," Lou muttered, but she nestled against me as if she was meant to be nowhere but here.

For a few minutes, there was nothing but the soft whisper of her breath and the muffled voices as Jasper and Quentin continued their half-hearted bickering. I let my other hand come to rest on her thigh, relishing her warmth and the smooth skin I could trace through her thin leggings.

"So, I made a good start," she said. "Where do we go from here? It's obviously not the last time I'll have to deal with the rogue underlings, and it's fairly likely the reps are going to get on my case again."

My chest constricted again with an instinctive urge to avoid the question. Yes, I was her only remaining tie to her criminal life—but it wasn't as if I had all the answers. Hell, I'd come to the totally wrong conclusion about things in the past, to the point of nearly making a huge mistake that would have upended both our lives.

Who was I to give any kind of advice?

Lou lifted her head to glance up at me, her brow knitting at my silence. I cleared my throat as if I were getting ready to reply.

I had to offer her something—the best I could. We weren't going to rush into action.

If it looked like I'd led her astray, I'd just have to bust my ass course-correcting.

"Let's see," I said to buy myself more time as I mulled it over. "With the Deadly Rose turncoats, I would probably give them a few more tests—chances to see if they'll stick to the loyal path or backstab you. If they pass, then you can trust them a little, but I still wouldn't let them find out anything particularly important like where we're actually living or training."

Lou nodded. "Gradually let them in, but never too close. That makes sense."

"There might be a point when you can bring them on board completely," I felt the need to add. "If they do something that puts your safety ahead of their own— you'll be able to tell when you can really trust them."

"If that ever happens."

I shot her a wry smile. "It might. That's how your latest skater won us all over, isn't it?"

The image of Quentin's bloody shoulder after he'd leapt in front of a bullet for Lou would never leave my mind. Mostly because *I* should have been close enough to defend her.

But I hadn't been and he had, so he'd earned his place by her side. All the more reason I should help her this way if she could use some strategy suggestions, though.

"That's a little different," Lou said lightly. Then her expression darkened again. "And the Devil's Dozen reps? What if they don't let up on me?"

I let out my breath in a ragged huff. "That's the trickier situation, for sure. You just keep telling them the truth as emphatically as you can… and I guess if they refuse to listen to words, at some point you'll have to turn to force."

Lou made a face. "Attack them?"

I shrugged. "We'd have to figure it out when we got to that point. A little strategic destruction to show you're not an easy target. I know you've got it in you when you have to go that far. But the whole time, the message should still be that your mother is the real problem and you're just trying to keep yourself safe and away from all of them."

"If only they'd listen to that. If they'd stand up to her, maybe we could actually live our lives freely. Imagine that!"

Her tone was wry, but it didn't completely disguise the longing in the words.

I hugged her to me. "We'll get there. Look at how far you've come in half a year. We're all the way on the other side of the world."

Lou let out a soft snort, but she hugged me back with her arm wrapped around my chest. "I really hope you're right. It's just intimidating going up against people who have as much power as my mom."

"The reps don't," I pointed out. "They're more like tangling with Sheeran in Boston, which you did just fine. And not all of the Devil's Dozen pricks are total cabrónes. Those two who were passing on info to you back in Austin seemed halfway decent."

Lou's head perked up. "That's true. I was so focused on getting away from everything to do with Mom and the Devil's Dozen that I didn't think about where Beckett and the Blood Hunter fit in. I should give the two of them a heads up about the threats I'm getting from their colleagues. They could speak up on my behalf—they know I was working against her, not with her."

I smiled at her, even though I could feel her already pulling away from me. She had work to do, and I wasn't going to keep her from it. "Sounds like you've got a plan —and a good one."

Lou leaned in to give me a lingering kiss on the mouth that made me wish I could strip the clothes right off her. Well, there was always later tonight for that.

"Thank you," she said with a sly smile that suggested she knew how she'd affected me. "For reassuring me and helping me figure things out. It's not something I'd ever want to do alone."

I squeezed her hand before she stepped away. "You'll never be alone, mi amada."

Now I just had to hold on to hope that I'd guided her well—and not into total disaster.

FIVE

Luciana

THERE WAS nothing better than hearing our coach's voice ring out from the stands as Jasper and I came out of our short program's ending pose.

"That was a really good run-through," Niko called from his bench. He'd been cleared to leave the hospital a couple of days ago, but he was mostly staying off his feet to avoid straining himself—a precaution the rest of us were strictly enforcing. "You've managed to stay on track even without my help."

I laughed, relief flowing through my chest. "We're a lot better off with that help, though." I glided over to the boards to grab my water bottle, Jasper following behind me.

Emi, who'd insisted on coming along to her brother's first few practices after his release to watch over him, clapped her hands in excitement. "I can't believe I'm getting to watch future world champions perfect their routine right in front of me."

My next laugh was a little shakier. "We're not world champions yet."

"And it's not *quite* perfect," Niko said, with a playful twinkle in his eye that made the critique he was about to deliver go down easier. "I think you could hit the footwork in that first sequence even more precisely—really nail that beat. And you pulled off the second lift just fine, but I'd like to see Lou get a little more height. You'll always be good that way."

I ran through the routine in my mind, absorbing his suggestions. "We can work on that. We've still got five weeks to polish everything up."

Emi cocked her head. "Are you going to keep the routines the same as from Nationals, or add something new to spice them up?"

Niko nudged his sister. "I think we're better off sticking with what we already know works. They've gotten fantastic scores with the current routines."

The rasp of blades against the ice announced Quentin's arrival. He'd been working through his own routines with an eye to next year's competitions, but now he leaned against the boards next to us and held out his phone. "I don't know. After you see this, you might want to rethink getting complacent."

Jasper shot him a mild glower. "I wouldn't call our routines complacent."

"Maybe not," Quentin said, agreeably enough. "But there's great, and then there's holy fucking crap. One of the guys I know who made it to Nagano for singles is practicing at the same rink as a couple of the pairs. He sent me this. Check out what the main Russian contenders for the gold are up to."

He turned his phone's screen toward us. Niko leaned forward, and Jasper and I studied the handheld recording.

A lithe blond woman skated next to a tall, broad-shouldered man whose darker hair was slicked close to his skull. They swept across the ice with perfect synchronization, grace radiating from their movements. Both strength and artistry showed as they whirled around each other.

"Okay," Jasper said. "They're really good. But what's the big—"

His voice died as the two skaters launched into matching triple Axels, hitting the ice at the exact same time. They circled around and immediately came together in a stunning lift that ended with… a quadruple Salchow throw.

My jaw dropped as the woman touched down without any significant wobble, one foot still lifted, even her hands at exactly the right angle. Holy fucking crap indeed.

"Wow," I said when I got my breath back. "That's—hardly anyone's managed one of those."

Jasper was staring. "Their form is good, they've got the creative aspects, *and* the technical difficulty on top of that… Their scores are going to be through the roof if they keep up that standard in the actual competition."

Even Niko was momentarily speechless. "I had no idea anyone was attempting a quad throw this year. It's usually considered too much of a risk… but they do seem to be up to the challenge."

Emi blinked hard. "OMG. That looked amazing." She shook herself and glanced between the four of us. "But, I mean, Lou and Jasper are amazing too. Is that really going to top their routine?"

"If they do everything right, most likely," Niko admitted. "I think that was their free routine, from the pacing. Ours doesn't have quite the same level of difficulty."

Quentin grimaced. "That's why I thought you should see it. If you *are* going to make any changes, you should get on with that ASAP."

I bit my lip, dread pooling in my stomach. I'd never assumed that we'd win at Worlds, but it was hard not to despair at the idea that we didn't even have a chance. "What can we do? I've got the throw triple Axel, but I can't land a quad Axel even in regular circumstances. I guess we could try to switch it out for our own quad Salchow…"

"Then it'd look like we're just copying them," Jasper said grimly. "No one's ever properly landed *any* other throw quad jump, so I'm not sure there's anything else we could switch to either."

Niko pursed his lips. "It is a different form too—you haven't done a throw Salchow at all before now. Have you ever done a regular quad?"

"No," I admitted.

"I'm not sure we could get there in just five weeks, then. And it wouldn't do you any good trying for something you won't achieve and ruining your routine over it. That's why quad throws are rarely done by anyone."

My hands balled at my sides. "We can't just give up. Those two could pull the throw off at the actual competition just as well as they did in that training video, and then we'd be screwed. What about the rest of our routine? There's got to be something. We've found other areas to ramp up the difficulty and the spectacle before."

Silence fell over our group. My stomach started to sink, but then Niko raised his head with an unusual firmness that spoke of total determination.

"There is one addition we could try that will make you stand out. You're solid with your death spiral and your lifts. You'd get more points if you went straight from one to the other. We'd need to rearrange the existing choreography a little, but only shifting a few moves around."

My pulse hiccupped. "Right from the spiral into a lift?" I *was* confident at both, but I was also fully aware that the death spiral got its name for a reason. It was one of the most dangerous moves we performed. As were the lifts.

They awarded big points for linking the two—but only because it was so freaking difficult.

Niko nodded in acknowledgment, but his eyes gleamed brighter as he gained enthusiasm for the idea. "It isn't often done either, but it's absolutely possible. It's also a better balance of points to difficulty than any other option I can think of. And you already have both pieces. With the time we have, I'm sure you could get there."

My mouth had gone dry. There was getting there in

practice and then nailing it perfectly in front of the judges. The former was a lot easier than the latter. If we failed during a performance, it could ruin the whole thing, just like Niko had said about the quad. Even attempting it could cost us any decent placement at all.

And that was assuming we didn't end up with a major injury on our hands before we even got to the competition.

But hadn't I just said that we had to give this our all? What was I here for if I wasn't willing to take that risk?

It wasn't any more dangerous than facing off with my mother's gunmen, that was for sure.

Jasper was watching me. "What do you think, Lou? You're the one in the most precarious position for both moves."

I squared my shoulders. "Let's give it a shot. What do we have to lose?"

Dios mío, let us not have to find out the answer to that question.

Emi let out a whoop and bobbed on her feet in excitement.

Niko waved us onto the ice. "Do some practice of the original spiral to make sure you're feeling totally confident in it. Think about how you'd need to adjust the exit to switch from it into a lift. I'm going to talk with one of my coach friends to see if she has any tips before we get right into it.

We ran through the spiral we were used to several times until I was dizzy. My brain kept cycling through the motion even when we were standing still. Niko motioned us over and gave us some suggestions about how to angle our bodies in the exit and quickly hit the right position for the lift.

Then we moved back into the middle of the rink. Quentin paused his practice to prop himself against the boards and watch.

I drew myself up straight and pretended my heart wasn't racing at a million miles an hour. We could do this. It was two things we'd already done, just pushed closer together. Piece of cake.

Maybe there weren't tons of pairs who'd pulled it off before, but a decent number had. I saw no reason we couldn't make ourselves one more.

We launched into the death spiral, my head whipping over the ice. Jasper's hand gripped mine as firmly as ever.

I counted out the beats, felt the shift as we transitioned into the exit, turned my body a little differently—

And stumbled before Jasper even had time to reach for me, let alone propel me into the air.

"Shit," I muttered as I caught my balance with my hand on the ice.

Niko applauded from the stands. "That was great for your first try. I can already see how it'll come together. Keep at it!"

The next two attempts had my temper fraying. No matter how much I focused on the new position, some part of my body wouldn't quite adapt.

On our fourth try, a spurt of anger honed my attention even more. I whirled around, landed in Jasper's grasp, and launched myself upward with his added propulsion.

Unfortunately, while I'd been busy getting the angle right for coming out of the spiral, I'd ended up off-balance for the lift itself. Jasper's hand slipped before he'd quite hefted me above his head.

I fell to the ice, his grasp only slowing my momentum. My hip still jarred against the ice hard enough to make me wince.

"Fuck, I'm so sorry," Jasper said, kneeling beside me. "Are you okay?"

I patted my thigh. "Yep. Just a few more bruises to add to my extensive collection."

I pushed myself to my feet, my breath coming ragged. Niko stood up, making my attention snap to him.

"You're supposed to relax," I chided him.

"And you shouldn't push yourself too hard either," he said gently. "That's enough for today. We can go for this change, but we have to be smart about it. It won't help either of you if you end up hurt."

"You were *so* close!" Emi exclaimed. "I know after a few more practices, you'll have it."

Jasper squeezed my shoulder. "I am pretty exhausted, Punk. We've got lots of time. I'll put together some new costumes too—something even more striking so our artistry is at another level too."

I swallowed thickly and forced myself to nod. Inside, my stomach had knotted.

New costumes weren't going to elevate us enough to make us gold contenders—not if we couldn't elevate the rest of our routine too.

Just how far over my head had I gotten myself, facing off against the greatest skaters in the entire world?

SIX

Luciana

I FLOPPED down on my bed and stared at the ceiling, but I just didn't have it in me to relax today. Our ice time didn't start for another couple of hours, and my thigh still ached from yesterday's fall, but I wasn't going to feel okay until we'd conquered that combined move.

With a muffled groan, I pushed myself upright and stalked into the apartment's living room. Niko was puttering around in the kitchen making tea, and Rafael sat on the sofa, scrolling through his phone. Jasper had gone off to find fabric for the amazing new costumes he had planned, with Emi volunteering as translator and guide. Quentin had asked to tag along, saying he wanted to learn from Jasper's expertise in that area.

The sight of Rafael on his phone sent a different prickle of apprehension through me. I stalked over and leaned against the back of the sofa next to his broad shoulders. "Has there been any news from the other apartment building?"

He shook his head without looking up. "Your mother hasn't launched any attacks there. And her rogue lackeys didn't take the other bait you gave them with that restaurant you mentioned you visited a lot, since she hasn't been terrorizing that place either. It doesn't look like the turncoats are passing on any information."

Somehow that didn't make me feel any better. I pushed away from the sofa to pace through the room. "So what am I supposed to do now? Even if they're not outright betraying me, that doesn't mean I can trust them."

Rafael set down his phone and raised his eyebrows at me. "Don't you have enough on your mind without worrying about that too? Forget about it until they do something that gives you an answer one way or another."

"Who says they're ever going to make a move that clear?"

"I do," he said with a hint of a growl. "Now sit down and relax for once in your life."

Oh, he thought he could boss me around just like that, did he? I set my hands on my hips. "If I wasn't the kind of person who takes charge and gets things done, we wouldn't be here at all."

Niko wandered over with a teacup nestled in his hands and a mischievous glint in his eyes. "I've heard of this concept called 'moderation' before…"

I made a face at him. "Oh, don't you start too."

He chuckled. "As your coach, I think I have even more

right to give you a few orders. And in my opinion, you need to stay focused on your routine and unwind between practices rather than overworking yourself."

I sighed. "We both know I can't totally forget all my other problems. They're pushing themselves into my life way too insistently."

Niko cocked his head. "I don't see any of them dancing around the room right now. It seems safe to stop thinking about them for a few minutes at least."

I glowered at him, but at the same time, I couldn't deny he had a point. "Why do you have to make sense?"

His grin widened. "That's my job as your coach, isn't it? To guide you effectively?"

Something about the amusement lighting his face sent a flicker of heat through my veins. I couldn't stop myself from licking my lips. "Were there any other ways you were thinking of guiding me while I'm supposedly 'relaxing'?"

"Hmm. I might be able to find a few techniques to help you loosen up..."

He set his tea down on the side table and slipped his arms around me. My head tilted to meet his kiss. Our mouths melded together with the same perfect sweetness they always had.

He was back here with me again. I wanted to revel in that fact. I wanted to melt right into him, but I kept my hands careful as I stroked them over his cheek and down his side, avoiding the stitched up wounds on his chest.

The floor creaked as Rafael stood. My bodyguard circled the sofa to join us, making my pulse thump even faster in anticipation.

"Don't think you get to be greedy just because you

caught a bullet for her," he rumbled, keeping his tone teasing. "This woman needs more than one man can deliver."

Niko eased back from me and grinned at Rafael. "If you think you can do better, then go right ahead."

Rafael loomed over me and dipped his head—to nip my earlobe rather than claiming my mouth. A squeak of surprise escaped me at the pinch of pain that brought a jolt of pleasure with it, and Rafael answered with an eager growl. He flicked his tongue along the crook of my jaw and finally planted his mouth on mine just as he slid his hand down to the elastic waist of the pajama pants I was still wearing.

A tiny moan slid between my lips. Rafael could always get me wet in record time. When he delved his fingers right beneath the thin fabric, my hips rocked to meet him, urging him onward.

"What do you think, brat?" Rafael murmured, loud enough for Niko to hear. "You want even more of this, don't you? You want both of us to carry you into your bedroom and give you the fuck of your life. Let's hear you say please."

His words sent a wash of heat through me. I couldn't deny they were true. "Please. Fuck me just right." I shot a glance over my shoulder at Niko. "Both of you. Ravish me."

Niko chuckled and stepped closer again. "Ravish, hmm? I think we could probably handle that…"

As Rafael captured my mouth again, Niko grazed his deft fingers over my chest to fondle my breasts. He pinched one nipple at the same moment Rafael circled his thumb over my clit, and I bucked in their joint embrace. A whimper tumbled out of me.

I couldn't forget that both of my men were still in recovery, even if Rafael was almost entirely healed. With a determined nudge, I directed us toward the bedroom. "This would be even more fun lying down."

Rafael clucked his tongue at me. "So impatient. But I do like a woman who knows what she wants."

As we passed over the threshold, he tugged off my pajama top. Niko didn't waste a second leaning in and lapping the peak of one breast into his hot mouth. I moaned and writhed with the pumping of Rafael's hand between my legs. My cunt throbbed with need.

For several seconds, we held there at the edge of the bed, too caught up in our shared desire to take the last couple of steps. Then Rafael slid his hand around to my hip and swept me right up to lay me in the middle of the mattress.

The two men clambered after me, and I clasped both of their shirts. "Off with these." I hesitated, my gaze lingering on Niko. "Or you can leave yours on if you'd rather keep the wounds covered up."

His smile turned only slightly crooked. "I'm not sure they'd be great for the mood. But I can strip down in other ways."

He reached for his pants. I openly ogled his leanly muscled legs as he exposed them, then switched to admiring the chiseled six pack Rafael had revealed.

My bodyguard smirked at me. "You look like you're enjoying the view. I certainly am."

I peeked at him coyly through my eyelashes. "I'd like you both to do a lot more than look."

Niko sank down next to me and trailed his hand down my belly. "You don't need to worry about that, Angel."

He tucked his fingers around my pussy to continue Rafael's work. Rafael chuckled and cupped my breasts. As he massaged sparks of bliss through my chest, he stole another demanding kiss.

My skin felt lit up with flames, heat flaring through my body from head to toe. When Niko curled his fingers right into my slit, I couldn't stop myself from crying out— or arching back against him. A second later, I froze, caught between my smoldering hunger and my concern for him. "I don't want to hurt you."

"I'm not that fragile," my coach reassured me, pressing an encouraging kiss to my shoulder. "Just don't flail around wildly, and we should be okay."

Rafael hummed to himself. "That sounds like a challenge."

A breathless giggle spilled out of me. "You can make me flail some other time!"

"Oh, I'm looking forward to it. Over and over again."

I shivered giddily and then let out another moan as he sucked one nipple into his mouth. Niko took the opportunity to lean over me and catch my lips with a kiss, still conjuring waves of pleasure between my thighs.

It was time I got a little payback around here. I groped for Rafael's sweatpants and slid my hand beneath them to grip his already rigid dick. His breath stuttered against my breast as he jerked into my grasp.

I stroked him up and down, and he sucked harder on

the nub he'd already turned achingly stiff. At my determined tug, he helped me yank the pants right off him, his boxers following quickly.

Niko took advantage of my distraction to peel my own pants and panties off me. Rafael eased down the bed as if the other man had unwrapped a present just for him.

He gazed up at me for just a second, taking in every inch of my naked body. His attention seared over my skin. Then he buried his face where his hand had been teasing me minutes ago.

He knew just where to nibble and where to slide his tongue over the most sensitive parts of my cunt. I gasped and squirmed against his mouth, but his hand held me firmly. All I could do was shake with the bliss building at my core, alternating between clutching at the short coils of Rafael's head and twisting my own head to meet more of Niko's kisses.

Niko took over up top, rolling my nipples between his fingers to thrilling effect. My head spun, but with the most fantastic of sensations. Mumbles slipped from my throat—I was pretty sure I was begging them to never stop, but I didn't care.

Rafael swiped his tongue from my clit all the way to my slit one last time and then rose up, leaving me panting for more. "Not enough," he muttered as he snatched at my bedside table, knowing I kept a box of condoms in the drawer. "I can never get enough of you."

He tore open the foil and rolled the contents over him at lightning speed. As he parted my legs, he simply rubbed the massive head of his cock over my pussy, glancing past me to Niko.

"I think you'd like to satisfy both of us, wouldn't you, brat? Do you think you can take Niko and me at the same time?"

A heady rush flooded my veins. I grinned. "I know I can."

Rafael grabbed the lube I'd also stashed in the drawer and tossed it to Niko. My coach groaned in anticipation as he squeezed a dollop onto his fingers. While Rafael pulled my hips closer to him, gradually guiding his cock into me with us both on our sides, Niko worked my back entrance over with practiced fingers.

It was easier adapting now that I'd done this a few times before. In less than a minute, I was swaying between the two men, whimpering for more stimulation.

Niko nipped my shoulder and lined up our bodies so he could stay lying on his side as well. Rafael raised my leg higher so my knee came right past his waist, and Niko pressed into me from behind.

My breath caught at the indescribable sensation of total fullness that I'd never get tired of. Rafael bucked into me, and Niko started up a rhythm of his own—a little more careful, but still forceful enough to have me crying out.

The combined thrusts sent my pleasure spiraling even higher. My vision hazed. The sound of my men's ragged panting and the sweat forming between our bodies only turned me on more.

"You feel so good, Lou," Niko murmured. "So right for me. You always do."

"So right for both of us," Rafael grumbled without any rancor.

All I could manage was a needy whine in response. My head tipped back, and my climax tore through me like a lightning bolt.

Niko's chest hitched, and I felt him follow me. With a grunt, Rafael pounded into me even harder. He cast me up, up, into the stars sparking behind my eyes and then groaned as he came.

We slumped together, our bodies sagging into the bed in the afterglow. I caressed Rafael's chest and rolled to nuzzle Niko's cheek, my heart full of endless affection for both of them.

"There," Niko said cheekily. "I kept up even with the bullet wounds."

Rafael gave a low guffaw. "And I'm sure you'll never let us forget it. You proved yourself well before this, Niko."

I made a light huffing sound. "What either of you deserve is based on a lot more than how good you are in bed."

Niko pecked a kiss to my forehead with a sly smile. "But it doesn't hurt our cases either."

Before we could fall into more playful banter, my phone chimed where I'd left my purse near the closet. My pulse hiccupped.

"That's the tone I programmed in for the Deadly Rose defectors."

Rafael shoved himself upright. "You'd better see what they want. It could be urgent."

As I scrambled off the bed, visions of a squad of gunmen swarming this apartment building swam through my head. I snatched up the phone, tapped on the message to open it up… and simply stared for several beats of my heart.

"Míerda! I can't believe— No. No, I totally can." My teeth set on edge.

Niko lifted his head, concern casting a shadow over his previously cheerful expression. "What's the matter?"

My mouth had gone drier than Death Valley. "None of us checked the news this morning, huh? It turns out someone defaced the arena in Nagano where Worlds is going to be held—just trashed the place."

"What?" Niko's eyes widened. "Who would do that?"

I raised my head with a grim smile, my stomach churning queasily. "Our new friends say they know it was people sent by my mom. A warning, or just a temper tantrum because she knows how important skating is to me. Either way, she's obviously not willing to let this vendetta go."

SEVEN

Niko

LOU STARED AT THE TELEVISION, raking her hands through the loose waves of her hair. The reporter on the news cast was speaking in Japanese, but the footage playing behind him made it clear what he was talking about. Imagery of Nagano's main skating arena, the doors bashed in, the light fixtures smashed and bent, and the walls streaked with crude spraypainted images slid by.

Lou let out a groan, one of many she'd voiced over the last several hours, and not the kind I liked to hear from her. "I can't believe this is happening. Threatening me directly is one thing. Now she's trying to fuck up the entire competition for everyone!"

Jasper came over and tucked his arm around her waist.

"It sucks, but you know your mother plays dirty. No matter what she does, it isn't your fault."

Lou threw her hands in the air. "I still have to deal with it. Obviously the March Wind and the Bright Dragon did shit-all to keep her in line."

As if on cue, her phone vibrated where she'd left it on the coffee table after several past calls. I leaned over to check the number and made an apologetic face at her. "That's another one of the TV stations. Looking to get a quote from you, probably."

Lou rubbed her arms and tensed up all over again when a clip from her and Jasper's performance at the US National Championships played across the screen. "Oh, crap. Have they connected the vandalism to me after all?"

I stepped closer to the TV to listen to the commentary. After a few sentences, I shook my head. "No, it's the same as before. They're talking about the shooting incident here in Tokyo as another example of recent crime in the skating world—saying how they haven't seen anything like this before and how it appears figure skaters have become a target for criminal activity for unknown reasons."

"If they figure out it was all the same person behind those crimes—and that she's my mother…"

I came up at Lou's other side and squeezed her shoulder. "There's no way they could find that out. You're not even using your birth name, and your mother doesn't advertise her real business anyway."

My phone chimed in my pocket. It'd been even noisier than Lou's and Jasper's since the story had broken nation-wide.

Quentin raised his eyebrows at me from across the living room. "You're awfully popular too."

I grimaced and ignored the text that'd come in. "I was the main victim in the first attack, and I live here. It makes sense that they're even more eager to talk to me."

But I had nothing useful to tell the reporters. I'd responded to the first several inquiries with brief remarks about how I was saddened by the incident but recovering well from my own assault. Normally I enjoyed talking with the media, but I was getting tired of it. These new texts I could wait to respond to.

Lou sighed and flopped down on the sofa. "I'm going to have to reply to someone eventually, right? What can I possibly tell them?"

Rafael came up to the back of the sofa and rested his broad hands there in a protective pose. "You don't have to talk to anyone you don't want to."

I sat down next to her. "He's right. But it might be good to pick one or two places to give a statement to. Why don't we wait a little longer and then sort through the requests? I'll help you pick the best venues."

Lou's shoulders slumped. "I still don't know what to say."

"You don't have to say very much," I reassured her. "Remember, they don't know that you're personally involved in the new situation. We'll decide together, but you can say something along the lines of how you want to stay focused on your skating and you trust the local police to find the culprits."

"Right." Lou exhaled in a slow stream. "It doesn't need to be anything more than that. I *shouldn't* say anything else. If I get flustered, I might give something away."

Jasper crossed his arms over his chest. "Don't forget that you've got nothing to feel guilty about. You didn't do anything; you didn't know it was going to happen."

I couldn't tell if she'd really relaxed. Seeing her so distressed made my own gut twist into an uncomfortable ball.

Before I could think of anything else to offer, my phone trilled with an incoming call. Restraining a groan of my own, I checked the call display, drew up a chipper attitude, and answered in Japanese. "This is Niko Okabe."

"Mr. Okabe," the reporter on the other end said in our native language. "I'm glad I could reach you. I assume you heard about the incident at the World Championship arena in Nagano earlier today."

"Yes," I said, repeating the words that were rote by now. "I was horrified to see it. Who would have thought skating could draw so much hostility! All we can do is keep training and hope that the beauty of our art softens the hearts of those who want to attack us."

"Well said, sir."

"Thank you. I should get back to my trainees…"

"Yes, yes, of course."

And then yet another exchange was over.

My phone let out another ring before I'd even lowered it, but this one was a different tone. I let out a soft chuckle. "That's Emi. I'll let her know we're all surviving the chaos."

I stepped into my bedroom where it'd be quieter and answered the phone. "Hello, little sister."

"Hello, big brother," Emi shot back in a typical playful tone. Then she got abruptly serious. "I just wanted to make sure you're holding up all right. I can't believe they're dredging up all that stuff that's ancient history."

My stomach sank. "What are you talking about?"

"Oh, no—you haven't seen—never mind—"

I sat down on the edge of the bed. "*What*, Emi?"

She let out a disgruntled sound. "It's on TXN now."

I grabbed the remote and turned on the smaller TV in the bedroom. The second I flipped to the right channel, my skin went cold.

My face filled the screen. A reporter's voice droned on in commentary, with far less emotion than I'd have said the story warranted.

"Though dramatic on the ice, earning gold and silver medals at multiple competitions, Niko Okabe has seen plenty of drama and scandal off the ice as well. One of the best-known incidents of his past involved a former partner of Okabe's, Kenzo Kiyama, whom the skater outed on live television as his boyfriend, followed by a hasty break-up and Kiyama's firing from his prestigious job."

Oh, kuso. Why in the world had they needed to unearth that old drama? Shame flooded my chest, nearly as sharp as it'd dug into me five years ago when my most epic screw-up had just occurred.

"That has nothing to do with the skating arena," I managed to say through my daze.

Emi huffed. "I know! And you were the victim in last week's attack—it's not like you were creating 'drama.' Are they trying to say that you deserved to get shot or something? It's ridiculous. I'm going to call the station and tell them so. But first—do you need anything? You or Lou or the other guys?"

"No," I said quickly. "Don't call—let the subject drop as quickly as possible. And we're all right, just a little frazzled."

"I bet. Try not to let any of it go too much to your head. You made a mistake once—it's not *that* big a deal. And if you do need anything, you know how to reach me."

"I do," I said dryly.

After Emi hung up, I sank back on the bed and stared at the ceiling. Lou's mother had managed to bring not just her past back to haunt her but mine as well. I liked the woman even less than I had before, which was a pretty incredible feat.

My phone rang with another unknown number. I brought it to my ear automatically, preparing my standard reporter response.

"This is Niko Okabe."

"What the fuck is wrong with you, Okabe?" a far-too-familiar voice snapped in caustic Japanese.

My stomach lurched. I jerked upright again, my palm turning clammy against the phone. "Kenzo?"

"Don't talk to me like we're still close. I'm remembering all too well why we're not."

I could easily guess what had gotten my ex-boyfriend so upset. The more unexpected part of this call was that he'd still had my phone number saved someplace. "I have no idea why the news stations are bringing up our history again, Kiyama. If I could do anything about it—"

Kenzo broke in with a scoffing sound. "You'll just fan

the flames even more. You can never get enough attention, can you? Five years later, and you have to drag my name onto the TV all over again."

Despite the weight of guilt in my gut, I couldn't help bristling a little at the accusation. "I told you how sorry I was when it happened, and I meant that. I definitely didn't *choose* to get shot or for the media to make a big deal out of the story."

"Sure. I know you, Okabe. You'll have played it up and encouraged them at every turn. Well, now you've gotten what you wanted. I just wanted to remind you that your selfishness affects people other than you. I hope you're happy with yourself."

"Kiyama—"

With a click, he hung up on me.

My voice died. My hand dropped to my lap, clutching the phone, and I simply stared at it for several heartbeats.

My insides felt as though they'd all tangled together. Shame still burned through my belly, but a spark of frustration had lit too.

I was sorry, and I hated that Kenzo was being put through the trauma of my previous actions all over again —and I had also been completely honest when I'd told him that I'd never wanted any of this attention.

His opinion of me had soured so much—and stayed sour even over the years. We'd had a joyful relationship before I'd screwed everything up. That one slip of my tongue had turned all the love we'd shared into total, unrelenting hatred.

As superpowers went, I could do without that one.

I swallowed thickly and tried to convince myself to get

up. I couldn't quite find the will to propel myself off the bed.

A knock sounded on the bedroom door, followed by Jasper's voice. "Everything all right in there, Niko?"

I opened my mouth to give another rote answer. *Yes. Of course. I'm fine.*

I wasn't fine, though. And I didn't want to lie to this man. I wanted to be better with both Lou and Jasper than I'd been with anyone before. Be open with him, let him in, make sure we were always on the same page.

How else could I make sure I never made such a huge misstep again?

"Not… not exactly," I admitted.

Jasper nudged open the door. When he caught sight of me, he kicked the door shut behind him and crossed the room in a couple of quick strides to sit down next to me. He leaned his broad shoulder against mine. "What's going on? It looks like there's more bothering you than just pushy reporters."

I pinched the bridge of my nose. "No pushy reporters. Well, none of them who're talking directly to me." I motioned to the TV I'd turned off. "At least one of the news stations has started bringing up other dramatic incidents I've been a part of in the past—particularly, the time when I outed my ex."

"Oh, shit." Jasper slid his arm around me as easily as I'd seen him offer the same affection to Lou earlier. Despite the turmoil inside me, something brighter lit up in my chest, melting a little of the anguish. "I'm sorry. I guess reporters can be sharks all over the world."

I gave a rough laugh. "That's not the worst part. My ex

saw and called to yell at me. He figures I encouraged the stories for more media coverage."

"What?" Jasper sputtered. "That's ridiculous. *I* know how awful you feel about that mistake, and I wasn't even there when it happened. How could he think that?"

"I did ruin his life in more than one way." I hung my head. "I can see how that would also have ruined his opinion of me. I tried to tell him that I never wanted it brought up again, but he didn't believe me. And then he hung up. I'm not going to chase after him trying to convince him."

Jasper let out a disgruntled sound and hugged me tighter. "He sounds like an asshole to me. It's one thing to be angry at someone in the moment, but to hold on to that much of a grudge years later—and take it out on the other person who's already shown how sorry they are…"

He scowled, which only made the fondness around my heart swell larger. "He has a right to his anger," I said. "And maybe I deserve to hear it. But it wasn't fun."

"No kidding. There's got to be a limitation on how long you can feel guilty over an honest mistake. He chose to live a double-life, with all the risks that came with it."

I didn't think Jasper fully understood the consequences Kenzo had faced. Both because things were somewhat different in Japan compared to the States, and also, maybe he'd never thought about himself being in the same position.

The moment that possibility occurred to me, I couldn't shake the idea. My mouth went dry, but I forced myself to look over at Jasper.

"Would you be all right if *our* relationship became

public knowledge? If a reporter found out and spread it all over the news?"

Jasper paused, but not as if he was bothered by the question, only as if he was thinking it over. He cocked his head. "I guess it might make our situation a little more complicated—raising questions about you as my coach and the fact that we're with Lou as well. But it's not totally unheard of for skaters and their coaches to get involved, and our professional arrangement is a lot more informal than most anyway. I think it'd be fine."

I blinked at him. "And you wouldn't mind people knowing?"

He shrugged and offered me a sheepish smile. "I'm not saying there wouldn't be any awkwardness. It's hard to know for sure when I've never been in that position before. But I don't feel any need to *hide* our relationship. I'm not ashamed of who I'm with—not Lou and not you either. We're really good together. That's something to be proud of."

Gazing back at him, at his beautifully crooked smile and the warmth gleaming in his gray-green eyes, I was lost in a momentary rush of affection. The same poignant emotion that had nearly spilled from my mouth that first afternoon in the hospital—that would have if he hadn't taken off in the middle of our conversation.

But I could say it now. He obviously wasn't going anywhere.

I beamed back at him. "I love you. More and more the longer we're together. I'm so glad that we managed to find our way back into each other's lives."

A blush spread up Jasper's neck to his cheeks. He let

out a rough chuckle. "I don't know if it was so much *finding* each other as you tracking me down halfway across the world."

Then his voice softened. He reached over to cup my jaw. "I love you too, Niko. Everything about you. *I* know you're one of the most selfless people I've ever met, putting other people's needs ahead of your own all the time. Cheering them up when they're down, putting in the work so that they can shine. You're something incredible."

With those last words, he guided my mouth to his. I gave myself over to his kiss, reveling in the eager firmness of his mouth, the contrasting gentleness with which his hand stroked down my side to my hip.

As he tipped me over on the bed, his fingers teasing up under my shirt now, the last knot of guilt released.

I'd fucked up in the past—massively. But I knew how to do better now. And I couldn't imagine anything as spectacular as the relationship I'd built with the woman on the other side of that door and the man who was right here with me when I'd needed him most.

EIGHT

Luciana

WHEN I EMERGED from my bedroom the next morning, my head felt stuffed full of wool, and I couldn't work the sour taste from my mouth. I found all four of my men gathered around the dining table, staring at an open laptop. Their gazes jerked to me, and their expressions made my stomach sink.

Bracing myself, I headed over to join them. "What now?"

They exchanged a glance, the skaters' gazes lingering on Rafael. He grimaced but shrugged as if to say there wasn't any point in trying to hide it.

Jasper turned back to me, his mouth tight with an unspoken apology. "The two incidents here in Japan have caught the interest of the international skating community. And they've been searching for new material to report on once they've covered the basics."

I raised my eyebrows. "So…?"

Quentin jerked his hand toward the laptop screen, which I could now see was open to a US news site. "They must have dug into the history of everyone who was at the rink when the shooting happened—which includes you. But all they had was your fake name."

"Right. That was the whole point—so they couldn't dig up anything incriminating." I hesitated. "What's the problem then?"

Niko reached over to give my forearm a gentle squeeze. "They haven't been able to find any information on you at all. No records of any competitions or even training and ice time under the name Luna Garcia before the past several months."

Jasper nodded. "Which means a bunch of reporters are now speculating about how it could be a pseudonym and why you'd have used one. Making up their own crazy stories about what your background might be."

My stomach plummeted. It was hard to imagine random reporters coming up with a past that was *worse* than my actual life, but that didn't mean I wanted them spreading their own stories around. "Shit. That's the last thing I need."

Rafael frowned. "For more reasons than your personal privacy. The Devil's Dozen pendejos didn't like that you were getting any media coverage at all. Reporters speculating about your dark secrets is *really* going to piss them off."

My heart stuttered. "Míerda. I hadn't even thought about that. It's a fucking awful situation all around."

Quentin braced his hands against the table. "I say we tell those assholes off. It's no one's business what Lou's been through."

Jasper rolled his eyes at his former rival. "Right. Because that'll totally get the news vultures to back off and apologize, not make them even more curious to find out what's up with her."

"I'd offer to take them all out for you," Rafael muttered, "but somehow I don't think that'll help put the rumors to rest."

I glowered at him. "I wouldn't want you to anyway." Queasiness wound through my gut, dispelling any interest I might have had in breakfast. "Maybe it was stupid to think I could get away with the fake name forever."

Niko rubbed my arm. "There was nothing wrong with wanting to keep a low profile and have people focus on what you're doing right now."

"That might be true, but trying to hide is what got us into this mess." I sighed and bit my lip. My stomach kept roiling, but from beneath the nausea, an undeniable truth rose up.

"I can't stay out of the spotlight anymore, can I?" I said. "They're going to be after me about my past no matter what I do from now on."

Rafael's muscles flexed as he crossed his arms. "You can ignore them. They can't force you to talk."

"They can't, but keeping quiet might look even more suspicious." I squared my shoulders. "I need to get used to this kind of attention. I wanted to compete on an international level, and this is what comes with the territory. I'm not giving up on skating, so I have to face the rumors head on."

Quentin cocked his head. "Which means doing what?"

I turned to Niko. "You helped me pick a couple of news outlets to give a quick statement to last night. Could you recommend a good show for me to do an interview on? Something that'd get enough coverage to reach everyone who's speculating?"

Niko wet his lips. "I could pick out a good option or two. Ones where they'd have someone with a good grasp of English on staff so it could be direct, too. But are you sure, Angel? You don't *have* to do this."

"No one should make you bow to the pressure," Jasper put in.

"I'm not bowing," I retorted. "I'm making the smartest career decision I can think of."

Rafael hummed to himself. "You voluntarily speaking to the press about your past could make the Devil's Dozen even more angry."

I smiled tightly. "That depends on the story I give them. I think I can spin a good one that gets everyone off my backs."

A glint of approval came into his eyes. "There's nothing wrong with showing the world you mean business."

I tipped my head to Niko. "I'm doing it. Set something up for me, as soon as you can get me in there."

❄

Stage lights glowed from all directions. Sweat had already broken out down my back, even though I was only standing off to the side of the main studio area. I swiped my clammy palms against my trim and professional-looking slacks.

I'd thought gliding onto the ice in front of high-level judges was nerve-wracking, but my skating competitions had nothing on this.

One of the program's staff caught my attention and motioned toward the small cluster of armchairs where the show's interviewer was waiting. That was my cue. I aimed a tight smile at her and strode out into the full glare of those lights on the set.

The interviewer stood by his chair until I'd sat down and beamed at me as he took his own seat. I could tell from the gleam in his eyes that he was hoping to get a juicy story tonight.

"Thank you so much for agreeing to speak with me and our viewers, Miss Garcia," he said, his Japanese accent only a little thicker than Niko's very mild one. "It's an honor to speak with such an impressive skater."

I forced my smile to relax as much as I could manage. "I'm glad to be here. I know there's been a lot of talk about me in the past couple of days, and I'm hoping I can clear things up."

"Of course. Why don't we start with the basics? I'd love to hear how you first became interested in figure skating."

This was comfortable enough territory. My smile softened even more of its own accord. "I fell in love with the beauty of the sport when I saw my first performance when I was five years old. Ever since then, I've spent every moment I can on the ice."

"Clearly all that hard work has paid off. I understand that this was your first year entering the major US competitions, and you and your partner, Jasper St. Pierre, placed first at the National Championships there."

I nodded. "That's right. It's been a thrill, finally getting to see my dreams through."

The interviewer folded his hands together on his lap. "And you're here in Japan now for the World Championships being held next month in Nagano. What are your hopes going into that competition?"

I couldn't restrain a laugh. "Obviously it'd be amazing if Jasper and I could win a medal there too, especially the gold. But what's most important is giving the best performance we can on the ice—giving it our all, no matter how we end up placing."

"An admirable attitude." The man paused and leaned forward in his chair with a slightly conspiratorial air. "Now, Miss Garcia, I believe the current concern is that you've presented yourself under a false name."

Here we go.

I swallowed thickly, doing my best not to let my expression stiffen. I wanted everyone watching to see a woman who was making the most of the hand she was dealt, who preferred to be honest and trusted her community to accept her.

It was a precarious balance. I needed to sound genuine, but I also couldn't risk getting *too* truthful.

My pulse thudded in my veins. I drew in a breath and

inclined my head. "Yes, that's right. I've been using an assumed name. But only for my protection."

The interviewer's eyebrows shot up. "Your protection? What have you needed protection from?"

My fingers twined together where I'd clasped my hands in front of me. I willed them not to clench so tight my knuckles would whiten.

The vague version of my story that I'd rehearsed spilled out of me easier than I'd expected. Like a valve opened to let the toxins flow out.

"It's my mother," I said. "I grew up in an abusive home. She was violent and mixed up with local criminals… I never felt safe there. It's been hard really feeling safe even after I ran off months ago."

The man's lips had parted in shock. Whatever answer he'd thought I might give him, it mustn't have been that.

Then he tutted disapprovingly. "Your own mother. That's very sad."

"Yes. I wish it hadn't been that way, but…" I shrugged in a "what can you do?" gesture. "The only thing I could control was how I handled it. I was scared that if I used my real name in the skating world, she'd realize where I'd gone and track me down. The last thing I wanted was to be found."

The interviewer's eyes widened. "I'm sorry that the recent news coverage may have made you feel as if you had to reveal all this now."

I shook my head. "It was bound to come out now that I'm competing on this level. I realized that I can't keep pursuing my dreams if I'm letting my fear of my mother hold me back. I just hope that whatever fans I have will support me in carving out my own, new life for myself."

"I'm sure they will," he said softly. "You mentioned criminal connections. Do you believe the recent incidents here in Tokyo have had something to do with your mother?"

"I can't say for sure." Which didn't mean I didn't know, only that I wasn't willing to admit it, but most people would assume I meant the former. "If either of them has been, I'm so sorry for any trouble that's been caused because of my family's associations. That's actually—there was a statement I'd like to make, if that's okay."

The interviewer swept his hand toward the main camera. "Go ahead, Miss Garcia."

I lifted my chin and gazed straight at the lens. My pulse kicked up another notch, but I focused on the idea of the people watching, the people I meant to speak to— every person in and involved with the Devil's Dozen, including Mom.

"I have no stake in anything my mother is doing these days," I said, firm and clear but allowing a trace of a quaver to come into my voice. I needed a hint of vulnerability for the benefit of the regular audience I wanted on my side. "I have no interest in any of her activities. All I want to do is skate—that's all I've ever wanted. Everything in my life is focused on my sport now."

I gulped another breath and continued. "So if anyone is trying to target me or other parts of the skating world because of who she is or things she's done, it won't get you what you want. You're coming after the wrong people.

Please, whatever you're looking for, leave us out of it. It's got nothing to do with me and my colleagues."

I finished with a bob of my head that I'd learned from watching graceful Japanese interviewees on similar programs. My mouth felt like it was coated in ashes.

Please, let those words be enough. Please, let everyone believe them.

"That was a very impassioned plea, Miss Garcia," the interviewer said. "Thank you again for opening up with us today."

I aimed my smile at him again. "It was my pleasure. I hope it does some good."

When the cameras cut for a break, the interviewer stood again to see me off, with a brief bow of his own. I managed to walk off the set steadily, but my legs felt like jelly.

The same woman who'd motioned me on led me to the room reserved for guests and their entourage. My men hustled over as soon as I stepped inside.

"We saw the whole thing," Jasper said, pointing to the TV mounted on the wall. "You were fantastic."

Quentin had his phone out, his finger swiping across the screen as he scrolled down a webpage. "People are already posting about the interview all over the internet. Lots of sympathetic comments. Seems like you won the regular folk over, at least, Upstart."

A laugh of relief slipped out of me. "Let's just hope it makes the right impact on the less regular viewers I'm hoping will see it."

Niko waved his own phone. "I've already been talking with the Tokyo police force. They're going to assign officers to keep us under protection—for the next couple of days while the story breaks, and possibly longer if it seems necessary."

My next laugh was rougher. "I guess that buys us a little security if the wrong people *do* take it the wrong way."

I'd played the hand I'd been given as well as I could. Would it be enough to get the Devil's Dozen off our backs?

NINE

Luciana

AS WE WALKED through the new arena to the edge of the rink, my skin itched with the impression of stares. This was the place in Tokyo where several of the other World Championship skaters had been training, a more prominent spot we'd felt we needed to accept now that we had so much more media attention aimed at us.

Mostly at me. I sat down on a bench to dig out my skates, trying not to think about the fact that the handful of skaters already on the ice no doubt were aware of all my dirty laundry now. Who knew what they thought of the newcomer who'd admitted to bringing chaos into their midst?

Or about the police escort my confession had earned me. Two officers had followed us in and stationed themselves in the low area of stands to keep watch.

I tightened my laces with hasty tugs. "Did we have to come during a freestyle session?"

Niko grimaced apologetically. "I couldn't get us in for any private slots until next week—and only a couple that week as it is. We'll have to mostly keep training at the other arena. But showing our faces here will mean fewer questions overall."

It made me more visible, but if anyone wanted to attack me, maybe showing up here would make them less inclined to go searching for my other training location. I could hope, at least.

Either way, along with the cops, Rafael was doing his usual patrol around the perimeter, watching for anyone with ill intentions.

As I straightened up, I caught one of the female skaters on the ice giving me a wary glance just before she jerked her gaze away. My stomach sank.

Then a jovial voice rang out, clipped by a British accent. "Hey, St. Pierre! I thought that was you."

A blond guy nearly as burly as Jasper came loping over. He grabbed Jasper's hand and gave it a hearty shake—I guessed they knew each other from past competitions.

"Good to see you, Andrews," Jasper said, shifting his weight awkwardly. "You always know how to find the best places to train, huh?"

"What's the point in skating around the world if you're not doing it in style?" The big man laughed at his own joke and nodded to Niko and me in acknowledgment, his attention lingering on me with obvious curiosity.

To my relief, Niko interrupted any further conversation by waving over an older woman with silvery hair. "Patricia! It's been a long time. Look, I've joined you on the coaching side."

The woman skated over on the other side of the boards with a light chuckle. "I heard. And from what I've seen, you've been doing great things with your first trainees."

Niko beamed. "They've given me excellent skills to work with. I learn as much from them as they do from me."

I swallowed hard, trying to clear the lump from my throat. The other coach didn't comment on the other things his skaters had brought to the table—like gunfire and vandalism—but I could guess what she was thinking.

I'd already felt a little out of place among the experienced competitors before. Now I couldn't help suspecting I stuck out like a sore thumb as someone who didn't belong. My voice stayed locked at the back of my mouth.

Jasper gave me a knowing look and grasped my hand. "We'd better get on with our practicing so we don't put Niko to shame," he said, and tugged me with him onto the ice.

When we found a section where no one was currently skating, I exhaled in a rush and eased closer to Jasper so I could speak under my breath. "I don't think we should try the new part of the routine here. I don't want anyone knowing about it earlier than they have to… and it's not like we have enough room to really stretch ourselves anyway while other people are practicing."

My partner nodded. "We'll have lots of chances to work on it at the other arena without worrying about anyone seeing us take a tumble—or knowing what we're up to. We'll only be here for a couple of hours anyway. Let's warm up and practice that footwork we need to speed up a bit."

We glided around in our normal exercises and then got Niko to put on our music so we could work through the footwork sequence. As I matched the movements of my skates to Jasper's, every beat echoing through the music, my awareness of potential stares faded away.

That didn't mean no one was shooting any more skeptical looks my way. But as I gave myself over to the sport I loved, I found I didn't really give a shit.

I'd already proven that I deserved to be here. Jasper and I had earned our gold medals at the US Nationals. This news story could be only a blip, and then people would be staring at us for much better reasons. The skating was all that mattered, and I still had that.

Jasper and I ran through the footwork until I barely felt my feet touch the ice and the music lived in my veins. Then we ran through several iterations of each of our lifts, every bit of practice helping ensure that we knew exactly how to stick the raised pose and the landing when it was time for the competition.

We were good at what we were doing. I could feel it. But what if it wasn't enough?

By the time the other skaters around us started packing up, the freestyle session almost over, hunger overtook my doubts. My stomach let out a forceful gurgle as Jasper lowered me to the ice, and he paused to catch my eyes, chuckling.

"Should we go get an early lunch? It sounds like you're going to go feral if you don't eat something soon."

I grinned crookedly in return. "I can make no guarantees about my temper when I'm hangry. I saw one of those conveyor-belt sushi places down the street when we arrived—want to check if it's open yet?"

Jasper rubbed his hands together. "Conveyor belt sushi it is." As we skated over to our bench, he cocked his head. "I guess we should pick up some takeout for Quentin too."

The other guy had opted to stay back at the apartment and sleep in, complaining that freestyle sessions weren't worth getting up for when he wasn't even competing.

A softer smile tugged at my lips. "Are you actually starting to get *friendly* with him?"

Jasper elbowed me. "Friendly? Kindly tolerating, maybe." But he was smiling too.

It warmed me inside to see the guys treating each other like family, especially the one guy who'd initially made their welcome particularly difficult. My good mood buoyed me as we filled Niko in on the plan and rounded up Rafael on our way out of the building.

We stepped out into the parking lot, my gaze swept over the city streets around us—and my feet stalled in their tracks.

On the other side of the parking lot, a man was just setting off toward us, his hands deep in the pockets of his wool coat. There was no mistaking the bright red hair sprouting from his jowly face.

It was the March Wind's man.

"Shit," I muttered, my gaze darting from side to side. "What does that prick want now?"

Rafael moved a little in front of me, his hand resting

on his concealed weapon. I carried out a brief internal debate and nudged him forward. "Let's go meet him. If this goes south, I'd rather it happened as far from the actual arena as possible."

I'd almost forgotten my new escort. The two cops had emerged from the building behind me. As I started forward, one of them made a brisk remark to Niko.

My coach turned to me. "He wants to know if this man is a threat."

My jaw clenched. The guy undoubtedly was, but not one I wanted the police interfering with if I could help it. That would make things ten times worse.

But that didn't mean I'd definitely be fine.

"Tell him I know him, and I think it should be fine. But they should keep an eye out just in case I'm wrong."

Niko passed on the message, and I hustled over to intercept the March Wind's man with Jasper and Rafael by my side. When I came to a stop by one of the parking lot's lamp posts, a few feet from the representative, I angled myself to the side so the cops would have a view of the unexpected arrival.

The March Wind's rep looked me over with a sneer curling his thick lips. I held my posture stiffly, my heart skipping a beat.

This was way too close to the parts of my life I wanted to keep separate from my past. Why the fuck had he needed to approach me here?

Well, I already knew the answer to that question. This was where he'd known he could find me. Maybe that was a good thing. They were finally figuring out I was actually serious about this skating thing.

"We need to have a little chat," the man spat out, his Australian drawl more pronounced in his apparent irritation.

I crossed my arms and answered his glare with a steely look of my own. "About what? I told you before that I've got nothing to do with any of your boss's business or my mother's."

The rep scowled at me. "The March Wind doesn't appreciate the public comments you've been making. The Devil's Dozen operates behind the scenes only. Any attention brought to it is a betrayal."

I narrowed my eyes even more. "It'd only be a 'betrayal' if I was still one of you. And I didn't say a thing about the Devil's Dozen. Or secret organizations or criminal masterminds. All anyone knows is that my mother is friends with some crooks. Sorry if that's not vague enough for you."

He bared his teeth. "It's not up to me what's good enough. If this is how you're going to handle your problems, we might just have to eliminate you from the picture once and for all."

Rafael let out a low growl. "That sounds like a threat. And I know exactly how to deal with threats to my woman. Are *you* looking to get eliminated?"

The man's stance went rigid, but he stood firm. "I'm just reporting the possible consequences."

Ignoring the clamminess of my skin, I wagged my finger at the guy. "How about the consequences of your boss's actions—or lack of action, more like it? I wouldn't have had to say anything about my mother if he and the rest of the Devil's Dozen had gotten her under control already. *She's* the one making public attacks that are obviously going to prompt the media to comment. I can't get away with saying nothing when she's forced my hand."

The March Wind's man let out a scoffing sound. "The thing is, between you and the Deadly Rose, it's a hell of a lot easier to deal with you."

He raised his hand from his pocket, a glint of dark metal showing, and my breath stopped in my chest. I jerked to the side instinctively—giving the watching cops an even better view of the goon.

Right—I had official backup here too. I tilted my head subtly toward the officers, holding the rep's gaze. "Really? Do you think the March Wind will be happy if you get arrested in broad daylight for pulling a weapon on a woman under police protection? Even if you manage to take me out in time before me and my men make you regret trying, you'll be going down too."

"But you're welcome to try," Jasper snapped, drawing his brawny frame up even taller.

The man's gaze darted from me to my men to the cops beyond us. He sighed sharply and slid his hands all the way back into his pockets. "I delivered the message requested. You'd better remember it. That smart mouth is going to screw you over someday, bitch."

Rafael shifted forward with a menacing loom, but the rep was already striding off toward his car. My shoulders sank as the tension rushed out of me with my next breath.

"Good riddance," I muttered. "What's next?"

Niko gave a laugh from behind us that only sounded a little strained. "I think now that you've dealt with him, next is sushi."

I managed to recover my smile. "Right. Let's get on with Mission: Fill My Stomach."

But despite my casual words, my gut stayed knotted as we headed off toward the restaurant, the cops trailing along behind us.

I was grateful for their presence and how it'd helped diffuse that situation. Things could have gone a hell of a lot worse with that asshole. But the problem he'd presented wasn't exactly finished.

Just how bad could this situation get before we could say goodbye to the Devil's Dozen forever?

TEN

Quentin

I COULDN'T RESTRAIN a low whistle as I followed Lou and Jasper into the fancy-pants new arena where they'd scored a private slot for the first time today. "And I thought the other place was nice. This is a top-level rink."

Jasper shouldered me teasingly. "Hope you're not too intimidated."

I guffawed. "Oh, I'll rise to the challenge, no problem." I cracked my knuckles and put on my best confident face even though my heart wasn't totally in it.

It was important to keep practicing. I wanted to be ready to blow everyone away when the next competition cycle started. But it was hard to throw myself onto the ice with full enthusiasm when I was surrounded by skaters who were getting to show off their skills on a stage I hadn't earned the right to.

Next year. Next year I'd make it to Worlds again. Anyway, I still didn't have total flexibility in my arm after the bullet wound that'd mostly healed. It was better to take things a little easy while I had the chance.

I'd just have to keep reminding myself of that.

The coach and skaters who'd had the slot before ours were just wrapping up on the ice. Lou and Jasper fell into a conversation about their twist lift, but when one of the guys stepped off the ice, Jasper waved to him. "Good practice, Andrews?"

The skater, who I vaguely recognized from the British team, shot him a jaunty grin in return. "Hopefully better than yours will be."

Lou tsked her tongue at him, her eyes gleaming. "Those sound like fighting words."

"It'll be a battle on the ice!" Andrews declared, chucking off his skates. As he wiped the blades, he glanced over at me and offered a more reserved dip of his head. "Wolfe, right? Quentin Wolfe?"

"Yeah," I said, and then just sat there awkwardly. We'd never really talked before—I wasn't sure we'd ever had much chance to. And Jasper had already asked the most obvious small-talk question.

The other guy loped by to the locker rooms before I needed to polish up my conversational skills. I guessed it wasn't really surprising that he hadn't tried to chum up with me. It wasn't as if I'd been particularly friendly with most of my competition over the past several years.

With *any* of my competition, really. Even the guy I

knew who was training in Nagano and had helpfully sent me that video of the Russian pair I could only really call an acquaintance. I was pretty sure he was more sucking up to me as a guy he saw as having good connections rather than wanting to show his appreciation for me as a person.

That was fine. There was nothing wrong with being practical—the skating world could be a cutthroat place.

But not as cutthroat as the world Lou had come from. As she and Jasper eased onto the ice, I looked down at the skates I'd only finished loosening the laces on and then across the stands.

Rafael was prowling around somewhere nearby. The current police escort of two cops were stationed in the stands. Neither of those facts stopped a prickle of apprehension from creeping down my back.

My practicing didn't matter that much. If anything interfered with Lou's… I hadn't taken this fucking gunshot for her harpy of a mother to ruin her chances now.

"I'm going to grab a drink from the vending machine," I called to Niko, who was standing near the boards. He gave me a salute, and I used the excuse to justify heading out into the hall for a brief prowl of my own. Call it a very basic warm-up to stretch my legs.

I didn't see anyone lurking in the arena's halls—or walking normally, either, other than when the last slot's skaters pushed out the doors right before I returned to the rink area. Their upbeat chatter trailed after me until the door thumped shut in their wake.

On the ice, Lou and Jasper were running through that twist lift, Lou spiraling in the air over Jasper's arms. I paused for a second, catching my breath at the spectacle.

Her mother was an idiot as well as a harpy. Even a total imbecile should be able to see this woman was meant to skate.

And I should be skating too. Trying to skate off the restlessness that was still gnawing at me, I sat down to pull on my skates, only for my phone to buzz with an insistent vibration.

Maybe it was my not-quite-friend in Nagano with more inside info. I dug the phone out of my pocket and checked the number, but I didn't recognize it. But then, I couldn't remember if I'd bothered to save him in my Contacts.

With Lou and Jasper's music bouncing off the high ceiling, carrying on a conversation in here would be a pain. I jogged back to the doors and slipped out into the hall before answering.

"Hello?"

A sharp, all-too-familiar voice penetrated my eardrum even though it sounded a little tinny with distance. "There you are, Quentin. Don't you dare get off the phone."

My heart lurched. Shit. After all the turmoil it'd taken to finally block Mom's number, it'd never occurred to me to worry that she might borrow a phone or pick up a new one to hassle me from.

I'd never had to worry about that before, but I should have been prepared. No one knew better than I did how relentless my mother could be.

"I'm here," I said tightly. "What do you want?"

"What do I want? How about an explanation for why it looks like I'm blocked from my usual phone? No rings, no text delivered, for *weeks*—this is how you treat your own mother?"

I gritted my teeth, my stomach twisting queasily. But I'd dealt with gangsters pointing guns straight at me—I'd taken a bullet that could have killed me. Mom didn't have anything on the hell I'd faced in the last few months.

"Maybe I blocked you because of the way you're talking to me right now," I retorted. "I'm a grown man—I make my own decisions about my career and everything else in my life now. Including who I want to talk to."

"Oh, and look what happens when you throw away my advice and motivation. You go off the rails with this crazy pairs stunt, disappear, get yourself injured and totally screw up your chances of competing on any level at all. You honestly think—"

I broke in before she could try to tell me how wrong I was. "I'll be competing just fine next cycle. It's only one year. No big deal."

She sputtered a laugh. "The boy I raised would never have given up like that. What the fuck has happened to my tough competitor, huh? You've gone all soft without me to keep you in shape."

"That's not the problem," I snapped. "If anything, you were dragging me down."

"Oh, that's rich. I'm the only reason you got anyplace at all. I kept at you and hauled you to all those practices and competitions, kept on your ass about performing right, and you were really getting somewhere. Now you're going and throwing away everything we built."

Anger seethed inside me, so potent I wouldn't have been surprised to find smoke pouring from my ears like some kiddy cartoon. "Everything *I* built. And the only thing I'm throwing away is you and your shitty attitude."

"Don't be so sure about that. I've got half a mind to fly out there to Tokyo and see if I can't get you back on track. You won't be hiding from me when I'm right there whipping you into shape."

An instinctive flinch ran through my frame, but no real panic followed it. The chances that Mom could pull together the cash for a last-minute flight to Japan were next to none. She was bluffing, stewing in her own venom like she so often did.

"Feel free to test that theory," I said. "I can ignore you just fine no matter where the fuck you are. It'll be easier for you if you take a hint and leave me alone."

I jabbed the End Call button before she had time to reply. With another few swipes and jabs, I'd blocked the new number too.

As I shoved my phone back into my jacket pocket, my stomach sank. *Would* she catch a plane all the way out here, just to complicate my already hectic life even more? It didn't seem possible, but I'd just underestimated her once.

God fucking damn it.

I stood there in the hall for several minutes, breathing deeply as if I could flush my mother's toxic influence from my head alongside the air from my lungs. It didn't totally work, but I started to get worried that the others would wonder what had happened to me.

Putting on my best disaffected expression, I walked back into the rink area and made my way to my equipment bag. When I looked over at the rink, Jasper and Lou were just launching into one of my favorite sequences in the routine—the newest lift that flowed right into a triple Axel throw jump.

Jasper spun Lou around with ease, not showing the slightest strain in the bulging muscles that I had to admit were more impressive than my own, and launched her into the air. She whirled in flight like the angel Niko always said she was and landed with perfect grace.

The talent that emanated off them sent a flutter through my chest—followed by a painful pang. They'd get to show that talent off in front of the whole world next month. And me… I'd be stuck on the sidelines.

What if Mom wasn't totally wrong? How much of what I'd worked so hard for *had* I thrown away to be here with this woman?

The hours upon hours of practice, all of the sacrifices I'd made from every other part of my life—would it turn out to have all been for nothing in the end?

How could I honestly say to anyone that I knew that it wouldn't?

ELEVEN

Luciana

"I CAN'T BELIEVE I'm saying this," Jasper said, around a mouthful of linguine, "but I think Japanese Italian food is better than the regular version."

Niko chuckled triumphantly, the sound pealing through the bright restaurant we'd stopped in for dinner. "I will eventually win you over to all things Japanese."

Jasper arched an eyebrow at our coach and poked toward him with his fork. "Don't say it."

"Even Calpis!" Niko declared.

I snorted with laughter, and even Rafael cracked a smile.

Quentin shook his head, unable to suppress a grin of his own. "You're just never going to give up on that quest, are you?"

Niko dug back into his spaghetti. "It's the most

honorable quest there is. But I guess I'll just be pleased that Jasper isn't feeling the need to pour maple syrup all over my country's cuisine."

I muffled another laugh. "This isn't even *your* country's cuisine." Although I had to admit there was something about the Japanese take on the seafood fettuccine I'd ordered that really hit the spot. For some reason I can't figure out, Italian seemed to be the most popular foreign food offered around Tokyo. Every mall had a floor of restaurants up at the top, and every one of those sort-of food courts included at least one Italian place.

Rafael grunted. "If you can find someplace in this city that makes authentic ropa vieja, then I'll be impressed."

Niko beamed at him. "I'll see what I can do."

I chewed my mouthful of prawn and tomato sauce happily, letting the cozy atmosphere wrap around me. There hadn't been many moments in the past few weeks when we'd been able to simply relax and enjoy ourselves. It was nice to forget all our troubles for an hour or two.

Of course, Rafael never stopped his periodic scans of the restaurant. We'd shed our police protective detail the last time we'd been at the big arena—I didn't want the cops knowing where we were living or our non-professional activities, and Niko had managed to convince them to stick to guarding me at that rink. For all I knew, Mom or one of her Devil's Dozen allies had hacked into the Tokyo Police computer system and would find out anything they committed to record.

Those crime bosses could insert themselves into almost any organization. I wouldn't be surprised if at least a couple of the officers themselves were on one or another

Devil's Dozen member's payroll. The criminal element in Tokyo would be under someone's domain, and they'd need ways of keeping the cops out of their business.

Quentin gulped down his last bite of chicken and cocked his head. "I could see spending more time here. If the rest of you were sticking around to keep some distance from the States."

Niko's eyes gleamed. "I'll have to get going with teaching you all how to speak the language."

Rafael guffawed. "Good luck with Lou. From what I heard, it was like pulling teeth getting her to even learn Spanish, and that's her family's heritage."

I wrinkled my nose at him. "My great-grandparents' heritage. Even Mom had to learn from tutors."

His voice fell into that teasing tone that never failed to get me all kinds of heated up. "I still think you could have a little more cultural appreciation."

I opened my mouth to give him a smart-ass reply, but a sharp trill from my phone cut me off. It was the ringtone I'd assigned to the trio of Deadly Rose lackeys who'd gone rogue.

The delicious flavors in my mouth turned to ash. I fished the phone out of my purse and yanked it to my ear. "Hello?"

Dámaso's thick voice carried through the line. "Luciana? Are you at the Sky Castle Mall?"

A chill washed over my skin. "How do you know that?" I hadn't talked to the defectors all day.

He swore under his breath. "We got a tip from one of our friends who's still working under Mireya—he's not ready to jump ship to your side yet, but he's hedging his bets. It sounds like someone working for your mom spotted you going into the mall, and she's sent a bunch of her people over to ambush you."

"Fuck." I pushed to my feet, my dinner forgotten.

"Yeah, exactly. Get out of there if you can. We're on our way over to see if we can help."

With that, he hung up.

My head spun for a second, but I squared my shoulders and willed down the worst of my panic. My men were all staring at me, Rafael braced like he could already guess what I was going to say. Which knowing him, maybe he could.

"My mom's people are heading to the mall to attack us," I said, snatching up my wallet to toss a handful of yen onto the table that should more than cover our meal. "We've got to leave—*now.*"

I didn't need to say anything else. The guys surged into motion like one being, as coordinated as any skating routine the three of them might have performed. They leapt up, and we hustled across the tiled floor to the glass doors, tugging on our jackets as we went.

I made a beeline for the elevator, my heart thudding. If the defectors had warned us in time, maybe we could make our escape before Mom's allies even got here.

Otherwise… things were about to get really messy.

The elevator car seemed to take years to arrive. We bolted inside, Rafael jabbing the button for the main floor. As the car whirred downward, he retrieved one of his pistols from its concealed holster and tucked it into his jacket pocket where he could keep it in his hand.

With a chime, the door opened. We hustled through

the wide hallway past the main-level stores, most of which had already closed for the night. The darkened displays gave the mall an eerie quality, but I had to be grateful for the lack of bystanders.

The broad front entrance came into view up ahead. I picked up my pace, my spirits rising but my hand dipping into my purse for my own small pistol, just in case. "Looks like we made it in—"

The words died on my tongue as about a dozen men shoved past the doors and marched into the building. In my first glance, I registered that a few looked like locals, but the rest were a mix of ethnicities. Maybe the criminal organizations here had gotten more diverse, or maybe Mom had sent over a bunch of thugs from her other territories.

It didn't really matter. Either way, these goons wanted us dead. The second they set eyes on us, all of them whipped out guns.

"Take cover!" I cried out, and threw myself behind the shelter of a vacant information booth.

The guys hurtled after me, Rafael firing off a few shots as he sprang. A grunt and a thump told me at least one of his bullets had hit its mark.

Other bullets thundered in our direction, slamming into nearby pillars and shattering display windows. I winced and peeked around the booth, my pistol ready.

The thugs were advancing on us. I wasn't okay with that.

I took a couple of shots, nicking one guy in the shoulder and sending another toppling to the ground, clutching his belly. Our other attackers jerked to the side of the hall where they could use the pillars as shields.

Quentin swore and pivoted on his feet, his own gun clutched uneasily in his hand. "Is there another exit we can make a run for?"

I followed his gaze and grimaced. "Not without giving those assholes a clear shot at us." The booth would only hide us from view until we got a little ways away, and then we'd have a sprint of at least a hundred feet before the nearest side hall.

"Then we'll just have to go through the pricks," Rafael muttered, and eased to the side to take aim at our attackers.

I followed his lead, but my next two shots only clipped the pillars. The gunmen launched another spray of gunfire our way, and I ducked back into safety.

"They won't just hang out there forever," I said through my constricted throat. "When they try to get closer, we'll have a chance to pick them off."

Rafael nodded, but his expression was grim. We'd have to take down an awful lot of them. And out of the five of us, he was the only one completely confident with his weapon. I knew how to handle mine from lots of practice, but it'd mostly been against unmoving targets.

Our lives were on the line. If the thugs closed in on us, we'd just have to do our best to mow them all down.

Niko wet his lips, his knuckles pale where he was gripping his pistol. He raised his phone to his ear with his other hand. "I'll call emergency services. If we can hold the stand-off for long enough, the police will deal with them."

My pulse stuttered. We didn't know how many of the cops we could trust—and I hated the thought of having yet another violent incident associated with me.

"Make it an anonymous call," I pleaded. "They don't need to know it's *us* getting attacked."

His mouth tightened, but he nodded.

As he spoke into the phone in soft Japanese, I peeked around the booth again. None of our attackers offered a clear shot. Shit, shit, shit.

Then three more figures burst through the front doors behind Mom's goons. My jaw dropped as I took in the three Deadly Rose defectors, all of them whipping up semi-automatics.

Dámaso's eyes glittered with a fierce gleam as he opened fire on the thugs, the mall lights gleaming off the lightning bolt shaved into his dark buzzcut. Frankie cackled and swung his scrawny frame around, pelting out more bullets. And as she squeezed her trigger, Ursula's straggly, bleached hair flew out behind her like she'd leapt into this reality from an action movie.

It only took an instant for our attackers to realize they were now under assault from both sides. Even as a few bodies crumpled, streaking the floor with blood, some of the other men spun, firing their weapons in turn.

The defectors hadn't given any thought to shelter. One of the first bullets tore across Ursula's elbow, making her arm jerk and the gun fall from her hand. Another slammed into Dámaso's chest, sending him reeling backward.

"No!" The cry tore from my throat, and I launched myself from behind the booth. As my finger squeezed the trigger over and over, my men followed me, adding their own bullets to the fray.

The arrival of the defectors had driven our enemies from cover. In a matter of seconds, with the sound of the shots booming off the high ceiling, the rest of Mom's men slumped to join their colleagues on the floor. My mouth tasted sour with adrenaline and revulsion; I couldn't tell how many were outright dead, or how many of the bullets that'd landed had been mine or Rafael's or even from the skaters.

There wasn't time to worry about that. I dashed towards the trio of defectors, shoving my gun back into my swinging purse. Ursula and Frankie had drawn close around Dámaso, Frankie pressing his hand to the wound on his friend's chest and Ursula clutching her bleeding elbow while she spat out hasty orders.

"Let's go!" Rafael bellowed, catching up with me as we reached them. "We'll get him bandaged up once we're out of here. If the cops catch us, we're all in deep shit."

Sirens were just starting to peal into hearing beyond the doors. We dashed through the entrance and across the courtyard outside, Rafael supporting some of Dámaso's weight.

We'd come by the subway, but racing down there amid all the regular civilians didn't strike me as a wise idea. Rafael appeared to feel the same way, leading us past darkened office buildings into a narrow driveway well out of view of the mall.

There, he paused for a second to whip off his jacket and tear off a strip of fabric to use as a bandage. I pawed through my purse. "I've got a roll of gauze and some pads."

As the other guys and I took over bandaging up Dámaso and Ursula as well as we could, Rafael took out his phone. "I think one of the contacts I've made here can get us medical care without drawing any attention. And hopefully a vehicle too—fast."

Dámaso forced his voice through clenched teeth. "I can keep walking—put more distance between us and the cops."

Ursula hissed a breath through her teeth. "Mireya's going to know we had something to do with getting you out. We should probably switch to a new building just in case she's already been tracking us down."

Looking at the two of them bleeding on my behalf, a lump rose in my throat. Rafael had said I'd know when I could trust the turncoats because they'd do something to prove themselves. If this wasn't that moment, then what else could they possibly do?

The words tumbled out before I could second-guess them. "You should come back to our building. We'll make sure you're all patched up and okay, and then we'll figure out a safe place for you to stay nearby. From here on, I think we should all stick closer together."

TWELVE

Luciana

TEN MORE PRACTICES, and we still didn't have the new transition down.

I spiraled and straightened up, collided with Jasper's arms and let him launch me into the air, but I could feel before I was even halfway up that both our positions were off. In our haste, he hadn't gotten totally centered behind me; I hadn't tilted my body at quite the right angle to achieve the height of the lift.

I swayed and Jasper's elbow wobbled, and he jerked me back down toward the ice before it turned into a total collapse.

"Shit," I spat out, swiping my damp bangs from my forehead. I'd stripped my long-sleeved thermal off an hour ago, but even my cotton band tee was clinging to my sweaty skin. The tremor that ran through my legs as I fought to steady my breath told me I wasn't up to a whole lot more practicing today.

Niko skated over, not a hint of disappointment in his sunny smile. "That was so close! Every time we come here, you get better."

Jasper sighed, rubbing his arms, which had to be at least as sore as, well, pretty much every muscle in my body at this point. "Close isn't going to get us any golds—or even bronze. At this rate, even if we do master it, we'll barely have any time to get comfortable with the full routine before we have to compete with it."

Even though similar depressing thoughts had been passing through my head, my stomach listed uneasily. "What are you saying?"

My partner grimaced but didn't hesitate. "I wanted this to work, but it's fucking *hard*, and you're already under so much stress. Do you really want to keep at this? The old routine got us this far. We could trust that it's solid enough as it is."

I swallowed thickly. "But we know it won't give us enough points to beat at least one pair if they don't screw up. For all we know, there are other teams with higher difficulty levels too."

"It's unlikely that many do," Niko put in. "Your current routine is already close to the maximum anyone would be capable of. And the more difficult moves anyone else is attempting, the higher the chances that they *will* screw up."

Jasper sighed. "Just like we're making it more likely that we will too."

He was right. I knew that. But a pang of resistance shot through my gut even considering giving up.

"If we go back to the regular routine, then we're already good with the whole thing," I said. "We don't need a ton of time to work on it. So let's keep trying the death spiral to lift transition for a few more practices and then make a final decision."

Jasper offered me a tight smile, sympathy shining in his gray-green eyes. "That sounds like a reasonable compromise. You never like to back down from a challenge, do you, Punk?"

There was nothing but affection in his words—and in his embrace when he tugged me to his broad chest. Niko eased closer to brush a kiss to the top of my head, and just for a moment, their love washed away all the frustration I was feeling.

"If anyone can do it, it's the two of you," Niko said with total confidence.

Jasper nodded and lowered his head to plant a kiss of his own on my lips. As he drew back, his smile softened. "I know that's true. No one should get between Lou and her dream."

I exhaled in a rush and flexed my arms in front of me. "I think *I'm* getting between myself and my dream today. I'm not sure I can skate another inch."

Niko clapped his hands. "Come do some stretches to make sure those muscles stay limber."

I glanced over to where Quentin was just coming out of a jump at the other end of the rink and then let my gaze slide across the stands of the private arena where we'd been spending most of our practices thanks to Emi's connections. A little more of the tension in my chest unraveled when I took in the empty benches. "I've got to say, it is nice to have the sessions here without reporters watching our every move."

As soon as they'd gotten wind about my new sessions at the bigger arena, news crews had started hanging around in the parking lot hoping to get a quote, occasionally even barging right into the rink area.

"I'll second that sentiment," Quentin called out as he glided past. "No news is good news."

In more ways than one. Obviously reports on the shootout at the mall had been splashed across every news source, but so far no one had connected what Niko said the Japanese media was calling "an organized crime incident" to me. No one had even known I'd been in the building… other than my mom, who obviously wasn't giving interviews.

Several outlets had still tried to connect the violence to the recent incidents in the figure skating world, though. A couple of reporters at the other arena yesterday had shoved microphones toward my face and asked with the aid of translators whether I had any thoughts on the new bout of violence in the city.

Wouldn't it be sweet if someday I really could skate without anyone focusing on the shitty parts of my past life? Hopefully that wasn't too grand a dream.

I shed those worries as well as I could while I stretched out my limbs. Quentin joined us for the last several minutes, and then Rafael fell into step with us as we headed out to the car. There was something comforting about having all four of my men around me, knowing I had every bit of their support, even if the rest of the world looked at me with skeptical eyes.

When we reached our building, I spotted Ursula casually standing guard on the sidewalk outside. She had her hood pulled low and a scarf tucked over her mouth to make her difficult to identify, but I'd expected to see one of the turncoats out here.

She dipped her head to me in a subtle nod as we drove by into the underground lot. Her coat hid all sign of the bandage on her arm.

We'd managed to score the three Deadly Rose defectors a small apartment on a lower floor of the building, a furnished space normally used by short-term business visitors. Which I guessed they technically were.

Rafael had managed to get a doctor to Dámaso before he'd lost a dangerous amount of blood, and the bullet hadn't punctured anything vital, so at least he was getting to recover in relative comfort. When I'd stopped by to check on them this morning, he'd been walking around the apartment, if with occasional winces. When I'd thanked him for helping save our lives, he'd only chuckled and waved me off.

"I don't know what *we'd* do if we were stuck with just Mireya to answer to. It was for my benefit as much as yours."

I wasn't going to complain about that attitude as long as it worked in my favor.

We were just stepping into the plain but cozy living room of our own apartment when my burner phone pinged with an incoming text. My pulse skipped a beat.

There were only two people other than the guys with

me who had this number. Neither of those two would be reaching out unless it was important.

My men all turned to study me as I pulled out the phone, their expressions darkening. We hadn't gotten a whole lot of good news by phone recently.

A text had popped up on the screen. My gaze skimmed over it. "It's Beckett—the Storm. He's asking to video-chat."

Quentin hustled over to the laptop we'd left on the kitchen counter after Jasper had been consulting it for recipes. "I can set that up. On the coffee table so we can all join in?"

From the other guys' stances, they definitely wanted to be included in the conversation. I nodded and hurried over to the sofa.

I ended up sitting in the middle with Rafael at my left, Niko at my right, and Jasper and Quentin perched on the sofa's arms. With a couple of quick texts, I passed on the necessary info to Beckett. Seconds later, an alert appeared on the laptop's screen.

When I tapped to answer the incoming request, a window expanded to show Beckett's boyishly handsome face, his ash-blond hair slicked back from his face like usual and a wry smile curving his lips. The guy didn't look old enough or harsh enough to have a place at the Devil's Dozen's table alongside people like my mother, but so far he'd seemed capable of holding his own.

"Hey, Lou," he said in a typically smooth tone. "How are you hanging in there?"

I nearly choked on my laugh. "I've been better. What's up?"

"I thought you'd want to know about some recent developments that affect you… Good ones, I think."

Most of my panic dissipated. "I'm all ears."

His smile turned a bit crooked. "You know the Blood Hunter and I appreciated that you exposed your mother's treachery rather than holding on to it for longer as leverage. You saved us a lot of time, money, and unnecessary bloodshed, and we don't like what we've been hearing about how the Deadly Rose has repaid you for that favor."

I made a face. "Yeah. My mom definitely didn't see it in a positive light. But it was the best move I felt I could make for myself too."

"Still, we were hoping we could balance things out and see that you get the recognition you deserve. Or at least the peace. The two of us and a couple of other members of the Devil's Dozen who your mother was gunning for have been pushing hard on the rest of the group to enforce sanctions against the Deadly Rose. Including penalties if she continues attacking you, since you acted in the best interests of the entire organization."

My heart leapt in eager surprise. "Seriously? Is there any chance the other members will listen?"

Beckett's smile stretched into a full-out grin. "Based on this morning's conversation with the full Devil's Dozen, opinion has swayed in our favor. We've gotten a few more members speaking up in favor of our motion, which gives us a majority. Your mother finally agreed to a ceasefire while we sort out appropriate restitutions and so on."

Quentin let out an approving whistle, and Jasper squeezed my hand.

My jaw had gone slack. "She's said she'll back off —completely."

"In theory." Beckett's eyebrows twitched upward. "Whether she'll stick to it remains to be seen. But if you have any more trouble in Japan that you think she's responsible for, let me know, and the Blood Hunter and I can send people over to assist. Now that we have an official agreement within the organization, we can act against her without it being a betrayal."

A startled laugh rushed out of me. "That's amazing. Thank you so much. I've been doing everything I can to keep her at bay, but obviously I don't have a whole lot of resources on that side of things."

Before I could gush any more gratitude, Rafael leaned forward to draw Beckett's attention. "Hold on a second. What about the rest of the Devil's Dozen? We've gotten threats from representatives of the Bright Dragon and the March Wind."

"They've mentioned their concerns about Lou's presence in Tokyo," Beckett said. "But the Deadly Rose ended up confirming that you really are there simply to skate, and they've said they'll withdraw any hostilities. Although again, if they go back on their word, the Blood Hunter and I will back you up against them too."

He spoke with total confidence, the assured air that made it easier to believe he was one of the most powerful criminals on the planet, but Rafael didn't look the slightest bit intimidated, let alone cowed. "What good is your help going to do us if you're on the other side of the world? If more goons start shooting at us, we're going to need backup immediately."

My bodyguard kept his voice firm too, without straying into outright aggressive. I couldn't help admiring his cool-headed response.

Beckett definitely didn't look offended. If anything, he was a bit chagrinned. "That's a fair point. I can arrange for some forces to be immediately on hand on neutral ground near Tokyo, and I'll send their contact information along as soon as they're in place."

"That would be a huge help," I said. "Maybe you could make sure my mom finds out that you're prepared to intervene directly, to encourage her to keep her end of the deal?"

Beckett chuckled. "I can definitely pass word along through appropriate channels."

"All right. Thank you again. If this works out, it's a huge weight off my shoulders."

"That's what I'm hoping for too. Thank *you*, Lou."

As I ended the video call, Rafael rubbed his hands together. "He thinks a lot of himself, but I get the impression he can back that confidence up. And that he means what he said. Not a bad ally to have."

I elbowed him. "Thanks for your vote of approval." I paused. "But really, it was good that you stepped in there. I was kind of overwhelmed by the news—I didn't even think it all through."

A ghost of a smile brushed across Rafael's lips. "I don't mind helping where I can."

I kicked out my feet, thinking the moment called for some kind of celebration, but before I could even get up, my other phone blared its ringtone. A groan spilled from my lips as I reached for it, followed by another when I saw the caller ID. "It's another news station. Probably another reporter digging for info."

Niko glanced over my shoulder and clicked his tongue. "You should probably talk to them. They're with one of the biggest stations. Put it on speaker, and we'll handle them together."

Restraining a sigh, I slid my thumb to the answer button. I'd just have to do what I had to do to get through all this drama.

No matter how people like Beckett stepped in, even if the commotion around the violence faded without further incidents… would I ever really be able to put my past completely behind me?

If I was going to stop this new life I'd built from crumbling, I couldn't hide in the shadows anymore, no matter how much I wanted to.

THIRTEEN

Jasper

HOLDING MY BREATH, I eased the fabric shears through the shimmering ice-blue cloth I'd spread across the dining table. It wasn't an ideal workspace, but it was the largest flat surface we had in the cozy but sometimes cramped apartment, though Niko assured us this place was spacious by Tokyo standards.

The cloth hissed as it parted in the wake of the blades. I didn't exhale until I'd reached the end of the line in the pattern I'd pinned to it.

I didn't know if we were going to pull off that new transition to elevate our routine, but I was going to make sure our updated costumes took even more breaths away. That much I could guarantee.

Lou was going to look like starlight shimmering off a

swath of frost. I could picture it perfectly in my head. Now I just had to stitch it all together.

Niko clicked his tongue against the roof of his mouth as he ambled over. "The fabric looks amazing."

I grimaced. "It's also a pain in the ass to work with. But it'll be worth it when I'm done."

He laughed lightly and leaned over to press a quick kiss to the top of my head, his slender fingers brushing over my neck in a caress. "I have no doubt about that. I'll leave you to it. Rafael wants to arrange a little more firepower for our new allies, and I think it'll go over better if he's got someone who can speak the local language along."

The bigger guy let out a huff from where he'd gone to the door to grab his jacket. "I'd let you go on your own if I trusted you to get a good deal for us. I don't like leaving Lou by herself."

Quentin aimed a narrow glance over the top of the sofa. "By herself? Hello, I'm right here."

"And so am I," I said, throwing a look of my own over my shoulder. "And aren't the Deadly Rose defectors taking turns guarding the front of the building and the hall outside our apartment?"

Lou raised her head from where she'd been stretched out on the floor, running through a workout routine. "They are. Not to mention that *I* can protect myself just fine all on my own even if I was by myself. Go do your negotiating. What did you train these guys in weapons for if you aren't going to trust them to use them when they need to?"

Rafael glowered at her before letting his gaze sweep

across the apartment in one more wary evaluation. "We'll be back as soon as we can. Call me if you need anything —*anything.*"

"Of course."

Rafael hesitated for just a second longer and then strode out into the hall. I caught Niko's friendly chatter starting up just before the door thumped shut, and my mouth twitched with a smirk.

I trusted Rafael to keep my boyfriend safe, but I wasn't sure how well the bodyguard would survive Niko's irrepressible good cheer.

Lou got up, shaking out her limbs, and let out a satisfied sigh. "I think I'm about ready for a nice, hot shower."

Quentin hooked his arm over the top of the sofa and raised his eyebrows at me. "I don't know about you, but I think that sounded like an invitation. We could heat things up plenty."

He grinned, his eyes gleaming slyly, and I found myself momentarily lost for words.

Part of me balked instinctively at the idea of going to Lou with this guy by my side. He'd been a *thorn* in that side for so long.

But he wasn't anymore. He'd shown how much Lou meant to him over and over. He followed her halfway around the world just to look out for her, for fuck's sake.

And there was no missing the fact that he was making the comment as a peace offering of sorts. He could have followed her without saying a word to me and made it a private interlude, just the two of them. Instead, he was holding out his hand and inviting me to come along.

Showing that he was both willing to share and willing to see me as an equal partner in the relationship.

I rolled the idea over in my head, my initial reluctance gradually fading. I'd gotten it on with Lou while Niko and Rafael were involved before. Why not Quentin? It wasn't as if I still felt any animosity toward him anyway.

Hell, there were brief instants now and then when I almost liked having the guy around.

I folded the draped cloth over the table and stood up, meeting Lou's gaze where she was waiting for my reaction. "I wouldn't mind offering a little… assistance."

Lou shook her head in amusement. "Well, come on then. If you're going to make yourselves useful, you'd better get on with it."

We'd given her the one bedroom that had an en-suite bathroom attached, us guys sharing the one off the hall— other than at times like this. Lou sauntered into her room with a sway of her hips I couldn't help tracking with my gaze, and Quentin and I trailed right behind her.

She stripped as she rounded her bed and made her way into the bathroom, tossing her shirt and bra aside and then wriggling out of her leggings without a hint of self-consciousness. Quentin followed her lead and tugged his own shirt off. I yanked at mine, not wanting to be left out.

By the time I'd chucked off my boxers, Lou had the water running, steam already billowing into the air. She glanced back at us, her gaze sliding over both of us with an appreciative gleam, but when her attention fell to her own body, her smile slanted on one side.

"That new transition has really been giving me a beating," she said, grazing her fingers over the purple-and-brown blotches that dappled the tan planes of her arms and legs. "I'm more bruise than regular skin."

When I caught the hint of uncertainty in her tone, the last of my self-consciousness fled. I stepped right up to her and skimmed my fingers down her sides, careful of the bruises that spread up over her hips.

"I think they're gorgeous," I told her honestly. "They're a beautiful map of the art you're working on creating."

Quentin let out a low laugh and approached Lou from behind. He set his hands on her waist just above where mine had stilled. "And they make you look like a total badass. Of course St. Pierre would leave out that part."

The trace of doubt had been slight—maybe she hadn't been insecure at all—but I saw her light up at the compliments regardless. With a mischievous smile, she grasped our hands and yanked us with her under the spray.

I had to say that despite the tight quarters, the Tokyo apartment made for easier shower-sharing than the locker room back at our old arena in Boston. Instead of a single stall, the movable shower head pointed its deluge over the entire—if smallish—bathtub. Which meant there was plenty of room for me to start soaping up Lou's shoulders and chest while Quentin got to work on her back.

As I cupped my hands around her breasts, she hummed happily, swaying between us. She trailed her hands down my chest, and my cock sprang to immediate attention.

I couldn't resist leaning in to kiss her. Her lips melded with mine, damp and warm from the water.

I wanted to sink right into her, but Lou had other

ideas. She tilted her head to nip my earlobe, and shivered as Quentin nibbled a path along her shoulder. Apparently he'd found just the right spot to spark her desire.

Carried by a competitive impulse, I massaged her breasts and stroked my thumbs over the soap-slick nipples. Lou arched toward me with a needy sound, and I claimed her mouth again with a sense of victory.

Quentin tsked his tongue behind her. "I'm going to need some of that sweetness too, Upstart." He grasped her thighs and tugged her back against him. From the pleased hitch of Lou's breath, he was hard enough to get her juices flowing too.

As she turned to face him so she could offer him a kiss, something twisted in my chest. But Quentin only let the embrace linger for a few seconds before cutting his gaze to me over Lou's shoulder.

"I've only got two hands here. I hope you're keeping yours busy—this woman deserves everything we can give her."

Not a competition—a collaboration. As I watched him tangle his fingers in Lou's hair with a brief jerk that brought an eager gasp to her throat, the twisted sensation smoothed itself out.

He had his own ways of pleasing her, of turning her on. Just like I did.

When we both worked together toward that end, it could only make a more spectacular experience for her, right? No one trying to do better than the other, but the two of us making the best possible moment we could for the woman we loved.

I palmed her breasts from behind and then slid one

hand down Lou's belly to her pussy. When my fingers teased over her mound, she growled impatiently and ground her ass against my rigid cock. My breath caught—and then stopped completely when she reached behind her to grasp my erection.

I muffled my groan by pressing my mouth against her shoulder just above the feathers of her angel wings tattoo. Lou smirked as she stroked me up and down and then moaned when I delved one finger right inside her. With a chuckle, Quentin captured her mouth again, winding his hand tighter into her hair and fondling her breast with the other.

He let out a hiss, and I realized Lou was working over his dick now too. His voice came out low and rough. "Fuck, you know how to pump me just right. Keep that up, and I'm going to explode."

Dirty talk had never been a particular talent of mine, but Lou appeared to enjoy it. She licked her lips. "That's the idea."

Her grip on my cock tightened, and I couldn't hold back my next groan. "God, I want to be inside you."

"You are." Her hips rocked with the motions of my fingers where a second had joined the first inside her. Her cunt was so hot and drenched with arousal beyond anything I could blame on the shower. The feel of her made my dick throb.

Quentin ducked his head to suck one of her nipples into his mouth, and Lou released a full-throated moan that practically had me coming in her hand. I clenched my jaw, struggling for control, and rubbed the heel of my hand against her clit in time with the pulsing of my fingers.

Lou writhed between us, her breath breaking into panting. "Fuck. *Fuck.* Enough playing around. I need you—both of you—on the bed. Now."

Neither of us was going to wait for a second invitation. I slammed the shower faucet off, and the three of us stumbled out of the bathroom in a tangle of limbs.

Our feet tracked wet footsteps across the floor, but I don't think any of us gave a damn. We tumbled onto the bed like one being, Lou grasping my cock again, my fingers teasing between her ass now, Quentin dipping lower to flick his tongue over her clit.

Lou gasped and bucked to meet him. I grazed my teeth along the crook of her neck, and she rolled toward me to yank my mouth to hers. The sheets bunched beneath us, already damp from our untoweled bodies.

We grappled with each other and our shared desire. Lou shifted position between us again and again, and all we could do was follow her lead. I dove in to suckle her breast and then to nip my way down her spine when she rolled toward Quentin again.

For a brief moment, Lou jerked away from us to fumble in her bedside drawer. She tossed a condom packet toward me and then lowered her head over Quentin's jutting cock where she'd gotten him sprawled beneath her.

My fingers closed around the packet, but my gaze stayed on them. I was getting a front-row seat to my woman delivering an obviously epic blowjob to the one guy I'd have expected to be most infuriated by.

Quentin's head sagged back against the pillows, his wet

hair fanning around his head. A flush had reddened his normally pale cheeks.

"You know just how I like it," he muttered. "Take it all, Lou, like only you can."

Should I have been horrified by the sight? Somehow after the intimacy we'd already gotten wrapped up in, not the slightest quaver of discomfort traveled through my nerves. The scene before me simply looked *right*.

Especially when Quentin opened his eyes a slit and aimed a pointed look at me. "Are you going to get on with getting her all the way off, or what?"

I could only grin at the playful challenge in his voice. "Hell yes, I am."

I'd never rolled on a condom faster. I lined myself up and plunged straight into my lover's slick pussy in one smooth thrust.

Lou cried out against Quentin's dick, the sound electrifying me. It thinned out into a low moan as I began to thrust. She was so wet, so tight as her inner muscles clenched around me—my mind blanked out, and my primal instincts took over.

I gave her my all, just as I would on the ice. My muscles drove my cock into her with every bit of their coiled strength, and the avid noises escaping her throat only urged me onward. I pounded into her, deeper with each stroke.

Quentin was swaying up to meet her mouth with his own rhythm. His eyes had rolled back.

He was close. I was right on the edge, careening closer with every second her pussy squeezed my dick. But we couldn't come without her joining us.

I slipped my hand beneath Lou to rub her clit. The sounds leaking from her mouth turned more urgent, and her pussy clamped tighter around me. Then she shuddered with the first ripples of her release.

The sensation propelled me with her. I came hard, my balls tingling, my vision whiting out with brilliant spots. The crash of ecstasy swept through me and left my breath ragged.

Quentin groaned as he joined us. Lou sucked his release down even through her own orgasm, moaning in approval.

I collapsed onto the soaked sheets next to her, glancing from her to Quentin and back again. "I think we might need another shower now."

All three of us burst into delighted, sated laughter. And just like that, it seemed ridiculous that I'd ever hesitated to join Quentin in this incredible encounter.

FOURTEEN

Luciana

SOMETHING about the morning light in Tokyo just hit a little differently. I sprawled under the covers, my eyelids at half-mast, watching the tiny dust particles float through the hazy glow of the rising sun like pixie dust.

It was nice to take a few moments to chill out amid the craziness of my life. For once, I could wake up slowly, and—

Just as I sat up with a luxurious stretch, my phone chimed with an incoming text. My regular phone, not the burner that Beckett or the Blood Hunter would have reached out to. And it was the tone I'd assigned to unknown numbers, my established contacts getting a different one, so it couldn't be any of my guys or the Deadly Rose defectors either.

My pulse hiccupped before I reached for the device I'd

left charging on the bedside table. Probably it was Mom trying to reach out again. She'd tried a few different numbers after I'd blocked the ones I already knew, and I deleted every enraged and unhelpful message without engaging.

As my fingers closed around the phone, I thought about calling Rafael in to check the message and delete it for me. Seeing her words wouldn't stress him out the way it did for me. But my gaze had already grazed the screen, and I paused.

No, I didn't think this was from Mom at all. The message was short enough for the whole thing to show on the screen: *Am I talking to Luciana Cordova?*

I stared at the text for a few halting breaths, debating my next move. Who the hell *was* it? Who would know my name and have my number, but not be sure it was mine?

Maybe it *was* Mom, and this was some weird trick?

I wavered in indecision for a minute longer before kicking off the sheets and pulling a hoodie on over my pajama set for warmth. "Rafael?" I called through the door. "You there?"

He answered in an instant, sounding as if he'd bolted to my room as soon as I'd asked. "Of course, Lou. What's up?"

"I need your help with something."

He eased open the door and strode in, worry clouding his dark eyes.

I hadn't meant to involve the other guys, but Quentin caught the door and peered in after my bodyguard. "Is everything okay?"

I waved him off. "Yeah. I mean, nothing's terribly wrong. I've just got to figure something out."

Quentin propped himself in the doorway, and Jasper wandered over too. I resigned myself to having an audience. I guessed the skaters had a right to know what was going on too… even if *I* didn't know yet myself.

I offered my phone to Rafael. "I got a text from an unknown number—but they seem to know who I am. I'm not sure if I should answer it."

Rafael scanned the screen. "You have no idea who this could be?"

I shook my head. "It's kind of like when the turncoats reached out to me, but at least they were more specific about how they knew my name and that they were on my side. This is so… vague, it could be anything from a friendly overture to a threat."

Rafael hummed to himself and pulled out his own phone. He checked the number against his own contacts, his frown deepening. "It's no one I've had contact with either."

Niko had joined the other two skater men by the doorway and obviously picked up on what was going on. "Could it have nothing to do with your criminal ties at all? Someone you knew at your school or another ordinary place?"

I rubbed my mouth. "That is possible too. Although I don't know why they'd be reaching out now either."

Jasper gave me a crooked grin. "Maybe they recognized you on TV from the competition broadcasts and want to reconnect now that you're famous."

I rolled my eyes at him, but the thought of possible

innocuous explanations settled my nerves a little. I exhaled roughly and glanced at Rafael again. "Do you think I should answer?"

He shrugged. "I don't see how it could hurt. Them knowing that they've got the right number doesn't give them any real advantage. And they might have something useful to say like the defectors did."

"Yeah." I hadn't really wanted to chicken out, and having him agree with my impulse to find out what was going on gave me the rest of the conviction I needed. "Here goes nothing!"

I took the phone back and typed out a quick response. *I used to go by that name. Who is this?*

I shifted my weight restlessly as I waited for their response. It only took a matter of seconds.

My name doesn't matter. I've got important information you should know about your close colleagues. Someone's looking to screw you over.

My heart lurched. "What the hell?" I looked over at the skaters while I showed Rafael the response. "They say someone I'm working with is going to betray me."

Rafael's lips drew back from his teeth in a silent snarl. "It's got to be one of that trio who came over from your mother's ranks. Shit."

I swallowed thickly. "I thought they'd done enough to show we could trust them."

"So did I." Rafael squeezed my shoulder. "This isn't your fault, Lou. They really pulled the wool over our eyes." He let go of me to pace toward the door and back, fury radiating off his stance. "But whoever it is, they're not going to live to see another sunrise."

His ominous words raised the hairs on the back of my neck. "We need to make sure we deal with the right one," I said, and tapped out another message.

Are you going to tell me who? It's not very helpful when you stay this vague.

Don't worry. I'll send you all the info you need.

I stood frozen as a series of images and videos popped up in the messages app. After a moment's hesitation, I tapped on the first image.

It was a screenshot of text messages between two people.

The bitch deserves everything that's coming to her, the first said.

No kidding, Rafe, the other replied. *There's no one better to get in there and do what needs doing.*

I'm going to make MC pay for what she did to my brother and every other fucked up thing she's pulled in this city. She'll have no idea what hit her.

The bottom of my stomach dropped out. I didn't know exactly what this was about, but it wasn't that long ago that I'd heard a gangster back in Austin call Rafael "Rafe." Was this something to do with him?

I swiped through a few more text messages that were more of the same: aggressive declarations from this "Rafe," encouragement from whoever he was talking to, and another reference to a "MC" who he was planning to savagely destroy.

Rafael loomed in front of me. "What is it? What're they saying?"

"I—I'm still trying to figure that out," I said, fighting to keep my voice from shaking, and tapped on the first of the videos.

A young black man with familiar coiled hair and broad shoulders was stalking back and forth in a dingy basement room. His muscles rippled through his arms as he appeared to pump himself up. "I'm going to smash that harpy into pieces. Tear the whole Cordova family down and stomp all over them until no one gives a shit about that name. They're never getting away with what they did to Edmundo."

Several other men were gathered around him at the edges of the frame. They let out whoops of approval. "That's right!" one of them shouted. "You get 'em, Rafe."

"She won't see it coming," announced the guy I could tell beyond a doubt was a much younger version of the Rafael I knew. "I'm going to get the bitch's trust and fuck her over before she has a clue she made a mistake. Take them down from the inside out."

"They fucking deserve it!" another guy hollered, and flung a knife toward a wall out of view. The camera swung to show a picture of a rose tacked to the wall, already pierced by a couple of other blades.

Rafael had gone still at the tinny voices when they'd first said his nickname. Now he lunged forward, snatching at the phone. "Don't— You can't watch that. It's not what you think. It's—"

I jerked backward so fast I bumped into the bedside table, making the lamp there rock. Hitting pause, I clutched the phone close to my chest, out of reach, and stared at the man I'd thought I'd known better than anyone in the world.

"It's a video recording," I rasped. "How could it be

anything other than what it looks like? You obviously recognized it just from hearing what you were saying. I think I'd better watch the whole thing."

Rafael's hands opened and closed at his sides. He took a step toward me, his eyes wild. "It's only going to mess with your head. You should listen to me *now*, not that shit from years ago."

I stared back at him. "I'll listen to you after I find out what all of that shit was. Or are you going to beat *me* down to take it from me like you apparently wanted to do to all the Cordovas?"

The color leached from Rafael's face, graying his rich brown skin. He didn't reach for the phone again, even as his eyes burned a plea into me. "It's only going to fuck things up."

"I've already seen some of it," I said. "I'd say things are plenty fucked up already."

When I was sure he wasn't going to tackle me for the phone, I sank down near the head of the bed and played the rest of the clip. And the next. And the next.

It looked like the recordings had all been taken pretty close together. Rafael's clothing changed, but his looks stayed pretty much the same, and his attitude kept the same vicious swagger. Whoever had filmed him had caught him ranting and raving about his brutal plans in continued detail.

By the time I let my hands drop with the phone to my lap, I'd heard him explain exactly what order he'd want to cut off various parts of my mother's body and which animals he'd like to feed those pieces to. I'd listened to him laugh about how easily he was going to insinuate himself within her ranks.

For several seconds, I didn't speak because I was afraid if I opened my mouth, I'd vomit. I forced myself to raise my head and meet Rafael's gaze. Behind him, the other three men were braced in shock in the doorway.

"It's true, isn't it?" I said. I didn't see how it couldn't be. "You started working for my mother so you could destroy her and her empire."

Every muscle in his massive body was tensed, and his face was etched with agony. His voice came out strained. "It wasn't like that. It *isn't* like that. I was young and stupid back then—I hadn't really thought through what it meant—"

I shot to my feet. "Don't give me bullshit excuses! You obviously knew exactly how you wanted to tear my family apart. You were planning that while you were watching over me, acting like you wanted to protect me when really…"

My throat closed up. A shudder ran through my body. I'd trusted him so much for so long without the slightest clue about how much rage he was hiding.

"I never hated you," Rafael said urgently into my silence. "I would never have taken it out on you, even at first. Lou, you have to—"

"I don't have to do anything!" I interrupted. All the anguish that'd welled up inside me threatened to spill out of me in a flood. Could I really have been so wrong— could I have put so much of my trust in a man who'd wanted to destroy everything I was…?

Fuck, fuck, fuck.

I didn't know how to wrap my head around it. I couldn't think past the thunder of my pulse while Rafael was right there in front of me, an echo of the vicious figure I'd seen in the videos.

I swung my hand toward the doorway, fighting to keep my voice steady. "I need you to leave. Get out of the apartment. I've got to have some space to figure this out. I can't decide what to think or what I'm going to do when you're here."

Somehow, Rafael went even more rigid than he'd already been. "Please, Lou. I swear, I'll explain—"

"Not now. It's too much. Just give me some room to breathe!"

Rafael stared at me and swore under his breath, but he turned and stormed toward the front door. The other men parted in his wake. He shouldered his way out of the apartment, and the door thumped shut behind him.

He was gone.

I'd drifted into my bedroom doorway to confirm it. When the front door stayed closed in his wake, I sagged against the doorframe. My thoughts swam through the haze in my head.

How could this have happened? How could any of this be possible?

But it was. I had more than enough evidence right here in my hand.

Unshed tears burned in my eyes. As I sucked in a ragged breath, my skater men eased in around me.

Quentin's jaw was tight, his eyes flashing with vehemence that matched his voice. "We don't need that lying prick. The four of us will do just fine without him."

I suppressed a slightly hysterical laugh. I didn't know if that was true. Rafael had done so much to protect me from the moment I'd fled Austin—both times.

Nothing about this situation made sense.

Niko slipped his arm around me. "We'll figure everything out, Angel. No matter what happens, we're here with you."

"That's right." Jasper touched my cheek at my other side. "You do whatever you need to do to feel safe. We've got your back."

I pressed my hand to my forehead. "I can't focus—it's all such a mess. I can't believe he'd have hidden something that *huge*..."

"Here." Niko guided me over to the sofa. "You catch your breath and give yourself time to sort through things. We'll make some breakfast. Everything is easier to take with a good meal in your belly."

The gentleness to his usual cheer only made me choke up more. He'd only known Rafael for a few months, but he could tell how much this revelation had rocked me.

As the guys hustled over to the kitchen to try to whip up some kind of culinary masterpiece that would fix my broken heart, I slumped over on the sofa. When I closed my eyes, fragments of the video footage replayed behind my eyelids, no matter how tightly I squeezed them.

My stomach kept churning. Maybe it was ridiculous. I knew my mother was a horrible person. I knew she'd hurt tons of people. I'd been willing to hurt her myself to get away from her.

But for Rafael to have kept this huge a secret from me for so long... For him to have been capable of putting on a false front like that to begin with… How much else had I misjudged?

How could I know whether any of the choices I'd made had been the right ones?

I'd thought I loved him. I'd thought he loved me. Could I trust even that much?

How could I say I loved him when I hadn't known such a vital part of why he'd come into my life at all?

My bleary gaze roamed around the room. Finally it landed on my skates where they leaned against my equipment bag near the door Rafael had just left through.

Other images rose up in the back of my mind, ones I didn't need a video of to remember them. All those years when Rafael had motioned me out the door with him and driven uncomplaining to the arena in Austin. The hundreds of times he'd stood guard in the stands while I skated for hours on end.

The quiet smile I'd sometimes spot after I completed a particularly difficult move.

All the attempts I'd made at flirting with him, starting back when I was no more than thirteen. The times I'd outright propositioned him—at sixteen, then eighteen— putting my heart out there on the line.

He could have had me. He could have taken my hopes, used me, and ripped me to shreds. Wouldn't that have made a perfect revenge?

But he hadn't. He'd resisted my advances every time.

And despite that, he'd never left my side when I needed him. He'd volunteered to trek across the continent with me without hesitation, even knowing my mother would be out for my blood and his. He'd come back to

Austin with me with the same threat hanging over him and done nothing that wasn't for my protection that entire time.

When I took everything I knew into account, I couldn't deny the facts. Even if Rafael had started working for my mother intending to betray her and tear down her empire, in the end he'd decided that supporting me was more important. He'd passed up all kinds of opportunities to undermine her so that he could look after me instead.

He was irreversibly interwoven into the journey that had brought me here—and I knew with a growing resolve that I'd come way too far to give up now.

But even with that certainty spreading through my chest, taking the edge off the pain, confusion clouded my mind. We couldn't go forward like this.

I needed to know exactly what had happened and why he'd wanted to hurt my family. Only then could I decide if and how I wanted to put the pieces back together.

I pushed myself upright on the sofa and glanced over at the guys in the kitchen. Savory smells drifted from the frying pan, but my mouth didn't even water.

"I think I'm ready to talk to Rafael some more," I said. "Get the whole story."

Niko nodded. "Whatever you think is right. You know him much better than any of us."

Jasper smiled tightly. "Yeah. We trust your judgment."

Quentin just scowled, but he didn't argue.

Inhaling deeply, I looked down at my phone and typed out a text to the man who'd been my rock for more than half of my life.

Come back? I'm ready to hear what you have to say.

FIFTEEN

Rafael

WHEN I REACHED the apartment door, I stopped. For a second, the burden of my omissions weighed on me so heavily I couldn't move.

All the secrets I'd kept from Lou.

All the casual deceptions I'd let myself pretend didn't matter.

All the horrible history that had brought us together, that hadn't gone away no matter how much I'd wanted to believe it had.

How the fuck was the woman I loved ever going to trust me again?

I wasn't going to find out unless I walked in there and talked to her. Even if she *never* forgave me, she deserved as much of an explanation as she'd let me give.

Girding myself, I raised my hand and turned the knob.

The door swung open to reveal an equally tense scene on the other side. Lou sat at the end of the sofa, one foot lifted to rest on the opposite knee, her back perfectly straight against the cushions. The other three men held themselves in a row behind her as if standing guard.

Niko and Jasper simply looked grim. Quentin outright glared at me. I could tell they were strung tight, probably ready to snatch at their weapons if I made a wrong move.

I couldn't blame any of them for their reaction.

Lou glanced at me with a cool expression. When she spoke, it was to the other guys. "I want to talk to Rafael alone."

Quentin let out a noise of protest, but before he could get any further into an argument, Lou held up her hand to stop him. "I'll be fine. Whatever he's got to say is about stuff from way before I knew any of you. I don't want any interruptions."

Jasper dipped his head, shooting me with a warning look. "We'll hang out in one of the bedrooms. Shout, and we'll be right here."

They headed off through one of the nearby doorways. As the door clicked shut behind them, Lou bent over and picked up the skate I hadn't noticed resting against the base of the sofa. She adjusted another object in her hand and brought the skate's blade to it.

Shrrrk!

I'd heard that sound dozens of times before. The sharp hiss of metal being sharpened against a hand stone. It raised the hairs on the back of my neck the same way nails on chalkboard might have, but I wasn't in a position to complain.

Lou didn't say anything to me, didn't even meet my gaze again as she angled her skate in rhythmic swipes across the stone. Honing the blade into just as much of a weapon as any knife she could have carried. I had no doubt that thing could slice through my skin if she wanted to cut me.

As she no doubt wanted me to be aware of while we had this conversation. A subtle yet unmistakable statement of her strength. I had to admire the gesture, even as it made my stomach churn.

She *had* said she wanted to talk. I took careful steps over to the sofa and eased down at the opposite end from her. She dragged the skate blade over the stone with another shrill scraping sound.

I let my eyebrows arch just slightly. "Should I be worried about whether this is a conversation or actually an execution?"

Lou's gaze flicked to me for just a second. "What are you talking about?" she said in a voice as smooth and cool as her expression. "I need to keep my skates in good shape. You know that."

"I do." I also knew that in this moment, she was every inch her mother's daughter. Not the awful parts that made the woman a vicious monster—the collected, professional aura of power that had made her a leader.

Lou could be a great leader too. Seeing her like this, I could imagine her keeping the Deadly Rose empire in line so easily.

If she'd actually had any interest in doing that.

What we were about to talk about now mattered to her. Keeping her self-control in the face of the potential threat I now might be mattered to her.

She didn't give a shit about world domination or racking up business earnings, and that was why she'd never be able to maintain the kind of authority her mother's heir would need long term. But she shouldn't have to.

She should be able to have whatever she goddamn wanted.

Not that long ago, that'd been skating, and the men she'd found on that journey… and me. More than anything, I wanted to pull her to me, wrap her up in all the protection I'd always offered, and show her she still had me.

That wasn't going to work. Not after what she'd seen. I had to use my words first.

Apparently it was up to me to start the discussion. That seemed fair too.

I swallowed my apprehension. "Lou, I'm sorry. More sorry than I can even say. I didn't tell you about any of that because none of it was true anymore. All the things you saw—they were from more than a decade ago. I haven't thought any of the things I said back then for a long time."

Shrrrk.

Lou kept her eyes on her skate. "But you did before. When you said it. You really did come to work for my mother planning to take her down, didn't you?"

"Yes," I admitted. "I thought I had a good reason to. The other guys you saw me with in the videos—they were part of my brother's old gang."

"The guys who confronted you in Austin? The ones who beat you up?"

"Yeah." I grimaced at the memory. "A few years after Edmundo brought me into the gang, Mireya lashed out at us what seemed like out of the blue. She killed my brother and a couple of other guys. I could barely wrap my head around living without him—I wanted to destroy the person responsible for taking him from me. The rest of the gang saw it as a flex of her power, just to show that she could and remind everyone to stay in line. Totally undeserved. I couldn't just accept it and shrug it off."

The pain of that long-ago loss prickled through me, dulled by time but not completely vanished. What would Edmundo have become if he'd lived? Who would he have been now?

The sad thing was, I wasn't sure it'd have been anything good.

I could have thrown away the best thing to have ever come into my life over someone who'd never truly earned that loyalty.

Lou had lowered her hand with the stone while I talked. She met my eyes with a pensive expression. "My mom did a lot of shitty things, but she didn't usually go around killing random people just for the hell of it."

"I know." I cleared my throat, trying to work the roughness from my voice. "At the time, I hadn't interacted with her at all, and I was reeling with grief and anger... I just wanted revenge."

Lou set down the first skate and picked up the other. She ran the blade over the stone, starting up the rhythm again. "And then?"

My heart sank with the memory. "After I'd been working with Mireya for a few years, working my way up through the ranks, I found out that it hadn't been random. Edmundo and the other two guys had tried to screw over a smaller gang in the city that we didn't know the Cordovas had a stake in. They'd killed a few people and stolen a bunch of merchandise."

Shrrrk. "And my mother retaliated with matching brutality. *That* sounds like her."

"Yeah. Reasonable retaliation." I shook my head, not knowing how to convey the full depth of my anguish to her—that I'd been so wrong, that Edmundo had made a move both so brainless and so heartless that it had nearly turned me into this spectacular woman's enemy. "I hate that I lost my brother, but as soon as I got the full story, I understood that it was his fault. He essentially attacked her first."

"But you stayed on," Lou said. "Why did you stick around if you weren't still planning some kind of revenge? I know you didn't *like* working for her."

"I didn't," I agreed. "I didn't like how she treated you or parts of how she ruled over her people... I had a bad feeling about the ambitions I caught glimpses of. I'd already been watching over you for more than a year then, and I could see you were better than her. I thought I'd stay, protect you and help you, and when you took over it could all be different."

"I guess you couldn't have gone back to your old gang empty-handed anyway."

My voice turned fiercer than I meant it to. "I didn't want to. I could see that I was doing something better by looking out for you. Even when you were a kid, there was something about you that shone through… It reminded me a little of my parents when they still had hopes for a better life. I couldn't abandon you and let her destroy that spark."

Lou let out a dry laugh. "So you stayed to wait for a preteen to ascend to her mafia throne."

I shrugged, affection clogging my throat as I thought of the girl I'd stayed for and the incredible woman she'd grown into. "It seemed like the best choice I had at the time. Although frankly, I'm happier here waiting for you to become a figure-skating superstar free of all that madness."

Her hand stopped, still clutching the stone. Her next words come out so low I barely hear them. "I'm happier like that too. Or I was."

That hint of the pain I'd caused her gutted me. I rubbed my hand over my face. "I should have told you sooner. After we got close. Given you the whole story so you'd know. But I—I didn't want you to think badly of me. I never thought I'd run into those cabrónes again, so it wouldn't matter. It could just stay in the past."

Lou put the second skate down next to the first and set the stone on the coffee table. Her hands clasped together on her lap. She looked down at them and then at me with so much hurt and determination smoldering together in her eyes I couldn't have torn my gaze away if I'd wanted to.

"I want to believe you," she said. "But it's so hard when you let me get blindsided like this… I need to know I can depend on you—now more than I ever have before.

Everything I've worked for—everything *we've* worked for —falls apart if I can't trust you."

The faintest quaver ran through her voice with the last sentence. She couldn't completely suppress the blow I'd dealt to her faith and her confidence. I closed my eyes against the urge to bash my own head in for fucking things up so badly.

But taking my guilt out on myself wouldn't help her. She'd just said it—she needed me. I just have to prove to her that her faith had been justified after all.

Violence came easy to me. That didn't confirm anything. I had to give her something that hurt me in a different way, that went against all my instincts... except when it came to the woman I'd have died to save.

My heart gave me the answer. I pushed myself off the sofa onto my knees and bowed my head before her, resting my forehead on her knee. Lou sucked in a softly startled breath. Her stance went rigid.

"You're the only one in the entire world I'd give my whole self over to, Lou," I said, putting all my devotion into every ragged word. "My strength, my pride, my life. There's nothing I wouldn't do if you asked. You could tell me to jump into a volcano right now, and I'd do it, because you asked."

A sputter of a laugh burst out of her. "I don't think it's going to come to that."

"Maybe it should. Because if you can't trust me again, if you can't bear to have me with you, then I have no purpose left. Every decision I've made, every step I've taken, for years, has been to serve you as well as I can. I made a mistake, but it *was* a mistake. I've got no secrets left. Please, don't make me give you up now."

Lou inhaled shakily, and then she was grasping my shoulders. As I rose at her tug, she wrapped her arms around me, leaning into the embrace I returned automatically with a rush of relief.

"I don't want to lose you either," she choked out, muffled by my shirt. "I was so afraid I already had."

I buried my face in her hair. "Never. You'd have to *throw* me into a fucking volcano to get rid of me now."

Another laugh hitched out of her. Then she pulled back, her dark gaze searching my face. "If you haven't had anything to do with your brother's gang in all that time, why are they attacking you? It must have been one of them who found my number and sent all that proof, right? Do they expect you to still get revenge on me and my mother—they think they can force your hand?"

I grimaced. "Probably. I did try to tell them the real story after I found out how Edmundo had screwed over Mireya's people, but they refused to even hear it. It was obvious they'd never accept the truth after they'd spent so long blaming her for it. Seeing me back in town set them off again."

Lou glanced at her purse, which no doubt held her phone. "Well, I can delete all that crap, and then it's gone."

"From your life. Not from theirs." Uneasiness prickled through my gut. "They exposed me to you—I don't know what they'll try next. They might manage to cause even more problems for you with your mother because of me. If they go to her with those videos, and she gets it into her head that we're scheming together against her…"

Dios mío, I couldn't even picture how much more of a terror Mireya would become with that idea fanning the flames of her rage.

Lou grasped my hand and squeezed it. "We won't let it get that far. We'll take them on together—like we have so many problems before."

SIXTEEN

Luciana

"UGH." I tried to restrain a yawn as I rubbed at my eyes, rocking with the bump of the rental car's wheels over a pothole.

Rafael glanced over at me from the driver's seat. "You never were good at sleeping on planes."

"Unlike you," I muttered. He'd drifted off in the seat beside me before we'd even left Japanese air space. I'd done my best to doze during the long flight back to the US, but I wasn't sure I'd gotten more than a couple of hours of very restless sleep.

I had to push through my fatigue and the jetlag, though. We had bigger problems in front of us—namely, the members of Rafael's former gang and the peace we needed to broker with them to ensure they didn't stir up even more trouble now that it seemed like my problems with my mother might finally be under control.

Fly in, have a quick chat, fly right back to Tokyo. Simple as that.

Ha.

Anton, the guy who ran the gang these days, had grudgingly agreed to our request to meet, as long as he could pick the location. We were heading into one of the roughest sections of Austin, no doubt smack in the middle of their territory.

My skin prickled with uneasiness, but the show of good faith had been necessary. They wouldn't have agreed to talk with us anywhere they thought we might be able to pull one over on them.

The one other time I'd met these assholes, they'd insulted me, accused Rafael of betraying them, and delivered a beatdown that'd left him in a cast and stitches. To say I wasn't looking forward to making any kind of deal with them was the understatement of the century.

But a girl had to do what a girl had to do.

Rafael eased off the gas as the grimy parking garage where the meetup was arranged came into view up ahead. "He's probably come with a whole horde of his goons."

I raised my chin. "That's fine. Whatever he needs to stay safe." I touched my gun in my purse and then the other in my jacket pocket. Rafael was armed too.

"You could let me handle it."

I shot him a narrow look. "It's my family they have the real problem with. Any way we hash this out, I've got to be involved. They need to know any agreement we come to is definitely from me as well."

My bodyguard sighed, but he didn't argue. We'd already had similar debates over the course of the past day while we arranged this impromptu trip.

He pulled into the shadowy cement fortress and parked not far from the entrance. Several figures shifted into view in the dimmer area toward the back of the structure.

I swallowed thickly and hardened my resolve. I couldn't afford to let any one of these pricks see that I was nervous. If they couldn't bring themselves to treat me as an equal, we were screwed.

About a dozen guys lumbered up to us, testosterone wafting off their flexed muscles and cocky smirks. Anton pushed to the front of the group with the broadest smirk of all, cracking his knuckles and studying us with his dark eyes.

"So, Rafe, you had the balls to come to us for once instead of making us track you down." He flicked his gaze toward me. "I'm surprised this one bothered to stick with you after she found out who you really are. I guess you really did win over some Cordova pussy."

A couple of his colleagues made crude gestures with their hips, and a laugh spread through the group. Rafael clenched his fists, but I touched his arm to hold him back.

Holding my stance firm, I rolled my eyes as if I didn't give a shit what he said about me. "I know who Rafael is now, unlike the bunch of you who seem stuck ten years in the past. After a decade, I think it's time we put this feud to rest."

Anton snorted. "Who are you to decide that, little puta? We still haven't gotten any payback for the shit your mother did. She thinks she rules this city, but we aren't going to bow down to any queen of *mierda*."

"No one's asking you to," I said evenly. "I don't work with her—I'm on my side, not hers."

Rafael tipped his head toward me. "It's true. Lou has completely separated herself from anything to do with Mireya."

With a sneer, Anton spat on the ground. "And we're supposed to believe that just because you said so? We've seen what backstabbing bitches you Cordovas can be."

A darker murmur rippled through the crowd behind him. He was getting his men riled up with thoughts of the supposedly unwarranted killings Mom had carried out.

But I didn't see any point in trying to convince them they were wrong about her. She'd done plenty of other awful things even if she'd been justified in taking out Rafael's brother. If these guys hadn't believed Rafael himself when he'd tried to tell them, they sure as hell weren't going to take my word for it.

We had to come at this from a different angle.

I clicked my tongue against the back of my teeth in a chiding sound. "Really? You do remember that I was only *eight years old* when your people were murdered, right? Are you seriously so pathetic that you'd hold a literal kid responsible for what her parents did?"

Anton's eyebrows shot up, but even as his eyes flashed, he couldn't restrain a grimace. The aggressive posturing of the crowd simmered down. Even these pendejos knew I had a point.

"You're not a kid anymore," one of the older guys snarled from where he stood by Anton's side.

Anton nodded with a jerk of his head. "Damn straight. And Mireya Cordova is even more of a tyrant and a terror than she was back then. You can't brush off your whole family history when shit is going down right now."

"I know she's gone off the rails," I said tightly. "She's been gunning for *me* too, as I'm sure you've noticed if you've been paying any attention at all."

Another gangster let out a scoffing sound. "You're still a Cordova. You've still got those ties."

Anton scowled at me. "You can't throw away all the responsibility for the family business when those riches will be going to you the second she kicks the bucket."

An edge I couldn't restrain crept into my voice. "I'd rather they didn't. I never wanted anything to do with the family business, and I'd be perfectly happy to see the whole fucking empire fall."

The man in front of me shook his head. His thugs rumbled discontentedly, skepticism stark on all their hardened faces.

We weren't getting anywhere just talking. I'd known making peace with just words was a longshot, but I'd wanted to give it a try anyway. Because the next step I was taking could come back to bite me if it didn't play out in my favor.

I glanced at Rafael. His jaw tightened, but he inclined his head slightly. We'd discussed what I'd do if I couldn't convince the guys to back down by verbally cutting ties with Mom.

So, I'd just have to offer concrete evidence of how little I gave a shit what happened to her.

I dug my hand into my purse, holding up the other

hand when the men stiffened. "No weapons. I've got something that'll actually help you."

I pulled out a wad of folded papers. Opening up one, I held it out so Anton and his men could see the lines sketched across it.

"I can give you the layout of the Cordova mansion. Every room, every hallway, every entrance, with notes about how they're typically guarded. I've got two more floor plans here, of a couple of my family's main business locations in the city."

Anton licked his lips. He gazed avidly at the amateurish blueprint and then back at me. "Why the fuck are you showing me that?"

"I'm making a gift out of it." I refolded the paper and shoved the bunch of them toward him. "You can do what you want with them. Consider it a gesture of trust. Now it's up to you whether you trust Rafael and me to stop my mother our own way and save you the trouble, or if you want to go at her head on if it's that important to you. You've got the option. It all comes down to how much you want to put your heads on the line."

"There's got to be a catch," someone muttered.

I shook my head. "No catch. I wanted you to see that I'm willing to let my mom get even more pissed off at me, if that's what it takes to prove which side I'm on and get *you* off our backs. We aren't part of your fight with the Cordovas. We're fighting our own battle. If you want, you can sit back and let us do all the work, but I'm not asking you to wait if you'd rather stick your own necks out."

The gangsters jostled against each other restlessly, their expressions flickering between eager and uncertain.

Anton rubbed his mouth and frowned down at the papers he'd taken before lifting his eyes to meet mine. "How exactly are *you* planning to finish her?"

Rafael grunted. "You can't expect us to give away information like that. You worry about what you're going to do, and we'll worry about our own tactics."

It would have been stupid to give them that kind of information anyway, when for all I knew they could turn around and sell it to my mom regardless of their past anger. But there was also the fact that I didn't have the faintest clue how the hell we were going to end her reign of terror just yet, which Rafael knew as well as I did.

A different voice rose up from the crowd. "How much time is it going to take you to deal with her, huh? How much longer are we putting up with this bitch lording it over us?"

With great effort, I avoided gritting my teeth. "We're doing as much as we can as quickly as we can. If I could get this all over with tomorrow, I'd go for it. But upending an entire empire takes time."

Anton shoved the papers under his arm and cast one more grim look at me. "We'll do what's best for us, then. Maybe we'll wait and see how your way pans out; maybe we'll just get on with things ourselves. But we can cut you and Rafael here a little slack."

I shrugged as if it didn't matter to me either way. "I appreciate that. The rest is up to you."

He spun on his heel, and his goons turned with him. They stalked off into the shadows they'd emerged from.

As Rafael and I hustled back to the rental car, I didn't

dare let my shoulders slump, even though I wanted to crumple in a mix of relief and trepidation.

We'd done it. I'd convinced the gang not to see me or Rafael as the enemy.

But I'd wanted more than anything to leave this part of my life behind forever. Now I'd made a commitment to staying with it until my mother was toppled from her throne.

And I had no idea how I was going to make that happen.

SEVENTEEN

Luciana

I MIGHT HAVE BEEN short on sleep, but we'd spent so little time in the US that stepping out of the Tokyo subway system into the crisp mid-afternoon air made me feel like I'd come home. My inner clock was back on the right schedule again, never having had a chance to switch over to across-the-ocean time.

I stretched my arms over my head with a yawn and glanced at Rafael. "The guys are probably training right now, but I think I need to sleep until tomorrow before—"

The trill of my phone cut me off—the ringtone I'd assigned to my guys. They'd have realized I should be in town by now. With a smile touching my lips at the thought of hearing their voices again, I dug out my phone. Jasper's name showed on the caller ID.

I brought the phone to my ear as I hit the answer button. "Hey! We just—"

"Lou! I don't know how long I'll be able to talk. We need help."

My partner's hushed but frantic voice crackled through the phone line. My pulse skittered.

"What?" I demanded, my fingers tightening around the phone. "What's going on?"

"We're at the rink," he rasped. "The smaller one. Your mother's people must have figured out we were training here. A bunch of men with guns stormed in—they've got us trapped in the stands."

My heart nearly lurched right up my throat. "What? She was supposed to—*fuck*."

A couple of distant gunshots rattled through the line. My pulse thudded even faster. "Have they hurt any of you?"

"No. Luckily the turncoats came along with us to practice, and they've helped hold the other guys off. But we haven't figured out how to reach an exit."

"Shit. We'll get there as fast as we can. Hang in there."

I shoved my phone in my purse and spun around, my thoughts whirling. Panic swept through my veins with its icy chill.

We were miles from the arena. I had no idea if we could get to them in time.

If I hadn't gone back to Austin—if I'd been there with them training, would I have seen a way out?

It might not have happened at all. Mom had probably picked this moment because she'd realized I'd left town.

No matter how hard I fought, the men I loved were being attacked from so many sides that I couldn't watch out for all of them at once. When was this going to end?

Rafael gripped my shoulder, his solid presence steadying me. "What's wrong, Lou?"

I blinked back the tears pricking at my eyes and strode forward, scanning the busy street next to us for a taxi. "My mom's people have attacked the guys at the arena. They've got them and the Deadly Rose defectors trapped by the rink. We have to get over there and give them backup."

Fury flashed in Rafael's eyes. "That maldita perra," he muttered, and sprang past me toward a cab that'd just pulled up to the curb to let out a passenger.

The second the passenger had walked away, Rafael dove into the front passenger seat. As I scrambled after him, he pointed his gun at the driver—low and careful with the safety still on, but that didn't make any difference to the guy, who stared at him with his jaw going slack.

Rafael spoke slowly and firmly. "I'm sorry. I'll leave the car for you to collect later. Right now we really need it. It's an emergency."

I had no idea how much the cabbie understood, but he didn't want to argue with a man with a gun. Leaving the key in the ignition, he bolted from the driver's seat, and I dashed around to take his place while Rafael re-holstered his gun.

"Was that totally necessary?" I couldn't help asking as I yanked the wheel to send the car back into traffic.

"No one's going to drive us there as fast as we need to go," Rafael retorted. "You put those daredevil skills to good use. I'm going to see what I can work out with Dámaso and the others."

He'd already swapped his pistol for his phone. As I wove between the other cars and hit the gas to fly through an intersection just before the light changed, his voice took on an even more authoritative tone than it had with the displaced cabbie.

"It's me. What's the exact situation there?"

He paused while Dámaso or one of the other defectors must have answered, and a couple of horns bleated their disapproval at my incredible driving maneuvers. My jaw clenched as I tore through another intersection.

Rafael nodded at whatever he'd been told, something about his unyielding posture beside me taking a little of the edge off my nerves. "That's not *too* many. Do you think there are more in the building? Okay. You know there's a back entrance, locked on the outside but useable as an emergency exit."

He fell silent for another longer stretch and then grimaced. "Fair enough. Listen, we'll burst in through the main entrance right behind these cabrónes. I want you six to move as close as you can to the upper hallway. Watch for the shooters to get distracted—run for it when you have the chance. Keep firing the whole time so they have to keep cover and can't take too good an aim at you."

He made it sound almost easy. Like he'd been giving orders in death-defying situations his whole life.

Well, he probably had. He might have been my main bodyguard, but he'd had to work with other members of my mom's security force on a regular basis. When it came to my safety, he'd had the ultimate authority over the rest.

"Stay on the line with me until then," he added. "I'll let you know when we get there. We're close now."

I tore around a corner and roared down the quieter streets of the wealthier neighborhood that held the arena. Somehow I didn't think *this* kind of attention was what Emi's friend had been hoping for when she'd made the deal to let us train there.

Could we possibly get out of this not only without any major injuries, but without making the front-page news yet again too?

The arena building came into view up ahead. I sped into the parking lot, wincing at the sight of a fallen security guard Mom's people must have picked off. So much for no major injuries. Míerda, this situation got worse by the minute.

I jerked up the parking brake, leapt out of the cab— and my breath froze in my lungs.

I could see through the broad glass doors that led into the fancy arena. And on the other side of the glass, cringing together with slim hands held over their heads while two gunmen pointed their semi-automatics at them, were three teenaged girls.

They had equipment bags at their feet—one had skates slung over her shoulder. School must have just gotten out, and these were the local trainees who used the rink, arriving for their own practice.

The men holding them hostage hadn't glanced over at us yet. Rafael shot me a determined look. "I'll go around through the back door. I can handle the lock. You keep them distracted, and then we go at them from both sides at once."

I nodded, my pulse now thundering in my ears. As he took off toward the back of the building, I headed toward the front doors, my fingers closing around the grip of the pistol in my pocket.

One of the men's heads jerked toward me. He pivoted, raising his gun, and I ducked into the shelter of a car parked just ten feet from the door.

"What the fuck do you think you're doing?" I hollered over the hood. "Those are *kids*. They don't have anything to do with me or this fight."

The guy shoved the door open to glower in my direction. "They're here. That means they're targets."

"You've already got plenty of other targets inside. Let the three girls go. There's no reason to keep them."

He let out a dark chuckle that raised the hairs on the back of my neck. "Your mother doesn't think so. She figures anyone who gets in our way is acceptable collateral damage. So maybe next time you'll think twice before you defy the Deadly Rose."

My stomach plummeted. I wanted to deny it, but I could imagine my mom giving the order all too easily. Even laughing at the thought of my distress at seeing innocent people dragged into our war.

She really had gone off the rails. She didn't care about the deal she'd made with her Devil's Dozen colleagues or the impact this rampage could have on her local connections. She'd gone fucking insane in her obsession with taking revenge on me.

And that made a woman who'd already been one of the deadliest in the world ten times more dangerous.

"I don't know why you're siding with her," I said past

the dryness of my mouth. Keep him talking—keep him from thinking about anyone else who might be approaching. "She'll turn on you as easily as she turned on me."

"Oh, I don't think so. Because I know when I've got it good, and I'm not going to bite the—"

His words cut off with two swift bangs. I lifted my head to see Rafael framed by the lobby's archway, his gun raised and the two men crumpling to the ground.

A couple of the girls shrieked. I ran over, holding my own gun low in the hopes I wouldn't traumatize them even more.

The guy who'd been threatening me had fallen between the one door and the frame, holding it open. I yanked open the other door, closer to the girls, and motioned them out. "There's no one out here. You can go home. Get somewhere safe! We'll handle the rest."

My urgency must have conveyed enough of my meaning even if they didn't understand my words. Their eyes wide with fear, they hefted their equipment bags and darted across the parking lot.

I met Rafael's gaze. He tipped his head toward the interior of the arena, where to my anguish I saw the security guard at the desk slumped forward in a pool of blood. But no one came running our way at Rafael's shots.

"I took down a couple of guys who were patrolling the halls—quietly enough that I don't think the goons in the rink area noticed," he said. "How about we take a similar strategy going at the last of them?"

I smiled grimly. "I distract them while you sneak up on them?"

"I was thinking more the coming at them from different directions. You can come out into the base of the stands through the women's locker room, right? I'll go through the men's. From what Dámaso told me, that'll put us on either side of them. They'll be nearly surrounded."

I exhaled in a whoosh. "All right. Let's do this before they realize something's gone really wrong for their friends."

I slipped through the locker room as quickly and quietly as I could. By the exit that led to the rink, I paused and listened at the door. No shots, only a couple of annoyed voices.

"We've got to get closer. The Deadly Rose wants them kaput."

"How d'you figure we're doing that without getting shot, you idiot? Let them waste their bullets taking potshots, then we go in for the kill."

Oh, he thought so, did he?

Scowling, I eased the door open just a couple of inches. Across the way, I spotted Rafael at his own door. He gave me a brisk nod from the narrow gap.

We shoved all the way past the doors in unison, each shooting at the men standing closest to us. The cluster of seven scattered—two, then three crumpling before they'd taken more than a couple of steps.

The other four bolted toward the ice. Rafael raised his voice in a bellow. "Now!"

More shots rang out from the other end of the rink. The gunmen jerked and collapsed. One flung himself toward the shelter of the boards, but Rafael strode to an opening and put a bullet in his head too.

My arm sagged to my side. I stared at the carnage we'd left behind, my gut churning.

"Fuck. This is a mess."

"I'll deal with it," Rafael said in his impervious tone. "I'll get the turncoats to help me take care of this and the taxi. You just worry about getting these guys home."

I found myself nodding automatically. He sounded like he knew what he was talking about—which, of course, he did.

He sounded like a leader.

A spark of an idea tickled up in the back of my head, but I couldn't pay attention to it when the men I'd left behind were hustling over to join us.

"Lou!" Niko exclaimed. "You're okay."

I caught him in a tight hug. "I should be saying the same to you." I turned to grip Jasper's and Quentin's arms tightly, my throat abruptly choked up. "I was so worried about you."

My gaze slid past them to the three defectors. Frankie was frowning, but Ursula held her head high, and Dámaso looked almost smug despite the bulge of his remaining bandages under his shirt.

"Thank you," I said. "You were amazing. Now we'd better get the fuck out of here."

As Rafael motioned the defectors over with brusque orders, my skater men and I hustled out to the rental SUV they'd arrived in. Quentin pushed behind the wheel, and I found myself tucked between Jasper and Niko, clutching them like I was afraid they'd disappear on me.

"She's not going to get away with this," I muttered. "She won't. I won't let her."

Jasper stroked my hair soothingly. "Hey, it's over now, Punk. I'm just glad we made it out in one piece."

Quentin glanced over his shoulder at a red light. "I'm looking forward to a time when I'm never getting shot at again, but it's not your fucking fault. Did things work out in Austin?"

My stomach knotted all over again. "About as well as we really could have hoped. I don't think Rafael's old gang will hassle us anymore, at least."

My mother, well... Who knew what hell she'd rain down on us next?

As the adrenaline seeped away, the idea I'd had before swam up through my scattered thoughts. I studied it, turning it over in my head as my confidence grew.

That... That wouldn't solve all our problems. Not even our most immediate problems. But it was one piece of the puzzle that I'd like to put to rest if I could.

When we got back to the apartment, all my body wanted to do was drop dead on my mattress. I forced myself to stay up, cuddling with my men and sipping tea, until Rafael walked through the door.

He dipped his head to me. "It's all handled. We'll need to do a little damage control with the arena management because of the security guard and the girls they scared, but we might be able to keep our names out of the situation."

Niko's head came up. "I'll start talking to them right away. Get ahead of the situation."

As he grabbed his phone and headed into his bedroom for quiet, I got up and grasped Rafael's arm. He let me pull him into my own room. When I turned to face him, his expression was solemn but curious.

"What's the matter, Lou? You don't look like you're hauling me in here to jump my bones."

An exhausted laugh tumbled out of me. "I think I'm too wiped to do that even if I was in the mood. Nothing's the matter. I've just—I've been thinking."

Rafael furrowed his brow. "About stopping training? You know that—"

I held up my hand. "No. I think that ship has sailed. We're on this course, no matter what comes. But I'm looking ahead to after things are more settled, and where that course might end up taking *you* too."

The furrows deepened. "What are you talking about?"

I drew myself as tall and straight as I could. "You know I've never wanted my mother's throne, Rafael. But someone needs to be the Deadly Rose. And I think you would make a much better heir than I ever have."

Rafael blinked at me, shock blanking his expression. "*Qué?* Lou, you can't really mean—"

The fact that the possibility had never even occurred to him only strengthened my resolve. "Of course I can," I interrupted. "It makes way more sense than me taking over. You've seen the problems with my mom's approach—and how it's gotten even worse. You want to make things better. You're a good leader. You know how to take command but also be fair, and you haven't lost your compassion, even if you know how to hide it."

He still looked bewildered. "I don't know. I never would have asked for anything like this."

I gave him a soft smile. "I know you wouldn't have. But honestly, if I get control over the Deadly Rose empire,

I'd hand it over to you in a heartbeat. If you're willing to take it. You should think about it."

I knew I would be thinking about it a lot… while I tried to see a way to wrench that power away from my mother before she destroyed us all.

EIGHTEEN

Niko

"PLEASE CONSIDER GIVING us a call back, Mr. Okabe," the reporter said as she wrapped up the voicemail she'd left me. "There's already a lot of speculation about how the recent shooting at the Sports Garden arena might be related to your attack and Ms. Garcia's family connections."

Beep!

Wincing, I set my phone down. In the past two days, the calls had been pouring in from both news stations and skating officials, and I hadn't had anything useful to tell any of them. The memory of cringing behind a bench, my heart racing faster than a bullet train at the thought of the actual bullets being fired, left my stomach knotted. And I wasn't going to admit to any of them that the incident was not only related to Lou but directly targeting her.

The worst wasn't even the nosy reporters. I could fend them off without any trouble—I'd been doing that ever since I stepped into the spotlight in my teens. But I'd generally kept on the good side of the professionals in our sport, even if they might have muttered about me behind my back from time to time.

The president of the Japan Skating Federation himself had left me a message this morning. His stern words lingered in my memory. *You still represent Japan even if you're coaching Americans. You should take more care in who you associate with. Think of what all these rumors are doing to our sport's reputation!*

That was the message I'd been getting over and over again from the skating world: my trainees were damaging the public's view of figure skating. The growing scandal was giving the wrong impression about what we stood for. Soon reporters would be eyeing all participants with more suspicious eyes.

And so on and so on.

What could I tell them? Yes, Lou had brought a lot of commotion with her, but it wasn't her fault. She was doing her best to put the horrors she'd experienced behind her and separate herself from that part of her life. Should she have been cut off from the sport she loved because of how other people were targeting her?

My phone pinged again, this time with a familiar custom alert. Emi. I snatched it up to see what she had to say after her talks with the arena owner.

As I scanned her message, my stomach sank.

Hey, big brother! I got everything sorted out with my

friend's uncle. He doesn't blame you guys for what happened… but he said he's not sure he wants Lou and Jasper to mention that they trained there after all, even if they win a medal. I guess I'll keep you up to date on that part.

With a sigh, I sagged back in the sofa. Now even the people who'd been most excited about our potential success saw us as bad luck.

Rafael's voice carried from the kitchen. "What's the matter? Are the reporters still hassling you?"

I lifted my head. The big man was leaning against the counter with a steaming mug of coffee in his hands.

I'd almost forgotten Lou's bodyguard was here. He had such a quiet presence despite his bulky frame. Jasper and Quentin had gone out after dinner to see about some finishing details for the new costumes, and Lou had crashed in her bedroom, still recovering from all her recent air travel.

I didn't like to set a gloomy tone, but I couldn't think of a single way to spin the situation into something worth celebrating. "It's reporters and officials and everyone else who has an opinion or questions. They all seem to want to paint Lou as the bad guy. I don't know what to tell them to get them off her back. But I can't have them getting into *her* head. She needs to focus on her skating."

Rafael ambled over to the living room and sank into the armchair. His mouth curved into a tight but wry smile. "I guess she's been building up her team of representatives so she can do just that. She's got you as her skating boss, and now she wants me to be her crime boss."

I'd caught a few remarks between the two of them over

the past couple of days that had given me the gist, but we hadn't discussed the subject as a group. "She's suggesting that you take over her mother's empire rather than her?"

He nodded, his mouth staying tight, his eyes going distant. "That's about the size of it."

As usual, it was difficult to read his reaction. "Would you *want* to do that?" I ventured.

His gaze came back to me, and he let out a dry chuckle. "That's a pretty important question, isn't it? Honestly, I don't even know. Obviously there's some appeal to having that kind of power, and knowing I could run things my way rather than her mom's... But am I really up to the full job? Just a few days ago, I almost lost Lou thanks to my past stupidity. My judgment is *better* now, but that doesn't mean it's perfect."

I'd rarely heard the man say so much at once. The decision must have been weighing on him a lot.

I'd also never expected to realize I had so much in common with the former gangster, even if we'd arrived at where we were from very different angles. Maybe it'd help him to hear that he wasn't alone in his doubts.

I glanced down at my hands and then back at him. "I think I know how you feel. I've had my share of epic mistakes. I once inadvertently outed my closeted ex on national TV and ruined his life." I waved toward my phone. "What if I end up saying the wrong thing again and damage the situation for Lou even more? That's the last thing she needs!"

Rafael took a long sip from his coffee, his expression turning contemplative. "I don't think you being too open about your past relationship has anything to do with how you'd handle Lou's career. It's not as if you know all that much about her past anyway, or that you'd ever think it's an important factor in her skating."

I paused, thinking that over. "They are pretty different situations. I mentioned my ex because I was happy being with him and wanted to share that happiness. There's definitely nothing to be happy about anything to do with Lou's mother."

Rafael gave a low guffaw. "Not at all. You've got to convince the officials that Lou is a great skater and not a liability, and that's what you already believe. Seems pretty straightforward to me, not much room for slipping up. Unless you were thinking you'd start pitching gunfire as a fun addition to the routine."

I couldn't restrain a snort. "No, there's no chance of that."

"There you go. You say what you mean, and that's what they need to hear, so there's nothing to worry about."

He sounded so confident that my nerves settled a little. He was right, after all. I wasn't hiding anything about Lou that I'd have wanted to say anyway. Everything I'd like the world to know about her was exactly the kind of things they *should* know to appreciate what an amazing athlete—and person—she was.

I smiled at Rafael, hoping I could return the favor. "You know, I could make a similar point when it comes to you. You made a big mistake years ago. But when you found out new information, you adjusted your mindset and took steps to fix things rather than sticking to the same course like the rest of your gang wanted to."

"I did what anyone should," Rafael muttered.

"But lots of people wouldn't," I said triumphantly. "Learning from your mistakes and being able to adapt and grow are things that don't come easily to a lot of people. But they are marks of a great leader."

Rafael opened his mouth as if he were going to argue and then paused. He frowned pensively before shaking his head in apparent bemusement. "Okay, you turned the tables on me. Maybe we're both being too hard on ourselves."

I grinned with the lift in my spirits. For a little while, faced with the barrage of accusations and requests, I'd felt alone and adrift. But we were a team—all of us, including Rafael.

We worked together in harmony, supporting each other, like any good relationship should work. The fact that we'd managed it even in one as complicated as ours was nothing short of incredible.

That's what we had here. Something totally incredible.

I picked up my phone. "I'm glad I could help—and thank you for your pep talk. Now I've got a couple of calls to make."

In the privacy of my room, I pulled up the number of the skating federation president. No time like the present to start setting everything else around us into harmony too.

To my relief, the secretary passed my call straight through. The president made a disapproving sound with his greeting. "It's good that you've finally returned my call."

"I appreciate you expressing your concerns," I said with all the cheerfulness I could summon. "I think there's a lot to say about Luna Garcia. Yes, she's come from a difficult past, but that means she brings a fresh perspective to the sport that we rarely see. Even in the short time I've been working with her, I can already tell she's going to transform figure skating in the best possible way…"

NINETEEN

Luciana

I SHIFTED my weight in the arena's bright yellow hallway, feeling like an elementary-school kid waiting to talk to the principal. Niko had gone into the manager's office alone to ask about booking rink time.

Beside me, Jasper glanced around the place. "I don't know if this is really our… vibe."

I grimaced. "We can't afford to worry about vibes. We can't go back to the Sports Garden arena now that my mom knows we've been training there, and there aren't enough slots at the big one to squeeze all our training in there. Even if we wanted everyone to catch on to the changes we've made to our routine."

"They're going to find out eventually," Quentin pointed out.

I shook my head. "It's bad enough us failing on our own without having a gazillion potential witnesses."

I still wasn't sure whether we should even keep trying the death spiral to lift transition. Our time before the competition was dwindling, and there'd been so many distractions. But I wasn't quite ready to let go of the hope that we could pull it off.

Neither was Jasper, apparently. He nudged my arm. "We'll find a place. If anyone can charm our way into some good ice time, it's Niko."

Quentin chuckled. "And if anyone can tackle one of the most difficult moves in skating, it's Lou Cordova."

Their affectionate encouragement lifted my spirits— which promptly sank again at Niko's expression as he left the office.

Our coach offered us an apologetic shrug. "He's booked solid for the next two weeks, which is the time we need it most."

Rafael and our newest allies were just sauntering over from a survey of the arena. The Deadly Rose defectors must have caught Niko's words, because Frankie propelled his tall but skinny frame forward with a scowl that pulled his cheek scar taut. "They don't have time, or they don't want to give it to Lou?"

A jolt of guilt jabbed my stomach, but Niko gave the gangster a mild look. "I didn't see any reason to think he was making false excuses."

Dámaso gave the hall a once-over. "The place doesn't seem secure enough anyway. Too many ways in and out."

"It'd be better than nothing." Frankie started to

swagger over to the manager's office. "Maybe if I give him a piece of my mind—"

Rafael pushed in front of the younger guy with a glower. "We're not here to intimidate anyone. We're doing this by skating rules, not street rules."

Frankie let out a scoffing sound, but he stood down, eyeing my bodyguard warily.

Niko waved to us. "Come on. There's another place we can try in the next ward over."

We piled into our two cars and drove over with Niko directing, but when we came into the next arena's reception area, the guy monitoring the front desk gave Niko a series of deferential but obviously discouraging gestures while he talked.

Ursula frowned. "What's going on?"

I hugged myself. "I don't know. It doesn't look good."

Niko turned back to us. "He says the manager is busy and can't see us this afternoon."

"Fuck that!" Frankie strode up to the desk. "Listen up. My man here needs to talk to the people in charge, and—"

As the receptionist backed up with a panicked expression, Rafael grabbed Frankie by the shoulder. "Tell him we're sorry about our 'friend' here," he said to Niko, and yanked the skinny guy over to the opposite wall.

His voice lowered to a growl. "We're trying to make Lou look *good* here, not like a terrorist. We don't want people associating her with criminal low-lifes, so pull yourself together and stop acting like one, or you can sit this mission out."

My face burned with embarrassment as I dipped it in

apology to the receptionist. But after Rafael's admonishment, Frankie did shut up, not even grumbling as he got into the defectors' car. Although he didn't exactly look happy.

After I'd slid into the back seat of our SUV, I raised my eyebrows at Rafael. "Look at you, stepping into the leadership role."

He met my teasing tone with a narrow look. "It doesn't mean anything. I haven't made up my mind about your offer."

"I'd vote for you as mafia king," Quentin piped up from the driver's seat.

Rafael sighed. "I'm still thinking about it." He brushed a strand of my hair back from my cheek with a stroke of his fingertips. "Let's say I'm giving it a try and testing out how I feel taking on a little more authority. We'll see how it goes."

I beamed at him and bobbed up to give him a quick kiss. "I can't ask for more than that." Then I gave the front passenger seat where Niko was perched a gentle kick. "Where to next, coach?"

Niko studied the list he'd made on his phone. "We haven't run out of options yet. And Emi is putting in some calls too. If I can just find someone who's impressed by my extensive star power..." He glanced over his shoulder to wink at me and froze as his gaze slid to the window.

My pulse hiccupped. "What?"

His throat bobbed with his swallow. "I think someone's here to talk to you."

I twisted around and found myself staring at the burly Asian man who'd spoken to us on behalf of the Bright

Dragon not long after Niko's attack. He'd obviously just gotten out of the sleek sedan parked behind him, and now he was sauntering over with perfect poise, his gaze intent.

"Shit." I didn't want to have a conversation with any of the Devil's Dozen people in the parking lot of some random arena… but then, I didn't want to have any conversations with them at all. I guessed this was as good a place as any. No reporters around snapping pictures. No fans or pro skating colleagues looking on.

Actually, that was probably exactly why the guy had tracked me down here.

Gritting my teeth, I motioned for Rafael to open the door so we could both get out. The other guys followed. Seeing us emerge, the turncoats clambered out of their own car to see what was going on.

As my men and my new allies gathered around me, the Bright Dragon's rep came to a stop a few steps away. His expression stayed cool but mild.

He hadn't been as much of a jerk as the March Wind's lackey. I didn't think the Bright Dragon had been on Mom's side. But that didn't mean he was on my side either.

When I'd reported to Beckett that Mom had struck again despite the deal she'd made with her colleagues, he'd been pissed—and promised he was going to take it up with his colleagues immediately. He'd also informed me that his men who he'd given me contact info for had moved their forces right into Tokyo in case I needed help quickly in the future. I had no idea if the Bright Dragon knew about any of that yet or how he'd feel about it.

My fingers itched to call in some of Beckett's people

right now for backup, but that might sour things faster when they weren't really necessary.

Instead, I propped myself against the SUV's trunk. "Fancy running into you here. Did you have something to say to me, or do you just hang out in random parking lots for fun?"

The rep held up his hands in a subtle gesture of peace. "Considering recent events, my employer felt we should have a talk."

"All right. About what?"

He cut his gaze toward the small crowd around me. "There are some things I'd rather not discuss in front of people who aren't part of our inner circle."

Before I could answer, Frankie stepped forward with a snort. "Oh, yeah? Well, we're her inner circle now, aren't we? After the way you dickwads have been treating her, you'd better give her and the rest of us some respect."

I whirled around. "Frankie, back off. I'm handling this."

He jabbed his hand toward the Bright Dragon's rep. "He's the one who should back off. These pricks are all the same, thinking they can bulldoze over everyone and call all the shots."

The other man's back had gone rigid, his eyes flashing with anger he didn't let seep into his flattened tone. "I can see my input is unwelcome here. I'll leave you to the counsel of your *wise* advisors then."

"Wait!" I shot a glare at Frankie and walked after the rep as he started to retreat. "He doesn't speak for me. I'm willing to talk. We're just all a little on edge after the constant attacks."

"Which *you* people have done shit-all to stop!" Frankie hollered before his voice cut off with a muffled grunt.

The Bright Dragon's man flicked one last dismissive glance my way. "You are who you associate with, Miss Cordova. You should remember that. We will. I've got better things to do than stand around being insulted."

He got into the sedan and jerked the door shut with a forceful thud.

Fuming, I spun around to see that Rafael had caught Frankie by the arm and clamped his other hand over the guy's mouth. As the sedan pulled out of the parking lot, Rafael let go.

"What the fuck were you thinking?" I snapped, marching up to Frankie. "He could have had something useful to say. He could have been offering an alliance to help keep my mom off my back."

Frankie scowled at me. "What do we need him and his stuffy boss or whoever for? It's not like they've done anything for us so far."

"That could have changed. You didn't give me the chance to find out."

"I told you to shut up," Rafael added, looming over the other guy. "If you're going to serve Lou, you've got to be able to follow orders—and recognize when she can handle a situation herself."

"Handle it herself?" Frankie sputtered. "These pricks keep coming at you. You can't make deals with them. At this rate—"

Rafael stepped closer, his gaze narrowed to a glare. "Now would be a good time to practice the shutting up."

"You've been going off half-cocked all day," I said,

setting my hands on my hips. "That's not how I do things. The whole point is that I'm *not* constantly on the attack like my mother."

Frankie shoved away from Rafael, throwing his hands in the air. "Fine. Fine! You think you'll get far playing things like that, talking down to the people trying to tell you the truth? Handle it your way, then. I've got better things to do."

Dámaso extended an arm toward him. "Frankie, come on, man—"

The thinner guy shrugged him off and stormed away. I stared at his retreating back, wondering if he even knew how to handle the public transportation in the city to get back to the apartment building. I guessed he could always hail a cab.

I restrained a groan. "Well, that went horribly." How much damage had he done with the Bright Dragon? Had he just made me one more enemy when I was having enough trouble fending off the ones I'd already had?

Rafael's expression had clouded over with different concerns. "We're going to need to find another apartment. We can't trust him if he's getting into moods like that— and we can't have someone we don't trust knowing where we're living."

My heart lurched. I hadn't even thought that far ahead. "You're right. Let's get back and move our stuff out right now. We can always stay in a hotel until we get something more permanent sorted out."

Niko brandished his phone, smiling tightly. "I'll get on that right now."

As we turned to our cars, Ursula touched my arm.

"I'm sorry," she said awkwardly. "He's been a hothead before, but I wouldn't have thought he'd go that overboard. He's just gotten real tense since the shootout at the mall."

Dámaso let out a derisive sound. "He didn't even get injured."

I heaved a breath. "We'll sort everything out. You two should pack up your things too. I'll let you know as soon as I figure out where we're going. And don't say anything to Frankie if he catches up with you there."

"Not a word," Dámaso promised solemnly. "He dug his own grave. He can deal with the fallout."

We scrambled back into our vehicles. Niko spent the whole drive making one call after another in animated Japanese, and announced just as we reached the apartment building that he'd found a couple of available short-term apartments in a place on the fringes of Tokyo. "Not as nice as this spot, but decent."

"The less flashy, the better," I said. "Okay, everyone—grab your stuff, and let's haul ass."

I don't think any of us had fully unpacked. I crammed my belongings into my suitcase, did a cursory sweep of the rooms, and hauled my luggage and my equipment bag down to the parking garage with my men at my heels.

My stomach stayed balled tight as we drove across the city to our new digs. We rode up in a plain but clean elevator to a three-bedroom apartment even more compact and spartan in décor than the last one.

But it was clean, and none of our enemies had any idea it existed.

We sorted out our rooms, and Niko, Jasper, and I

ducked out for a quick grocery run. Niko handed off the defectors' keys to Ursula on our way down. When we made it back to the apartment, Rafael looked over our acquisitions and decided he could whip up some kind of dinner with them.

As the smells of boiling rice and sizzling garlic laced the air, I sagged onto the hard sofa and released some of my tension with a sharp exhalation. "Let's not do that ever again."

Quentin grabbed one of my feet and started massaging the arch. "Hey, at least it's over now. We got out before that idiot could screw us over any more than he already had."

Niko let out a crow of excitement from across the room. "I found us a rink! One of the places I reached out to this morning says they had a cancellation and can fit us in now."

A startled but pleased laugh tumbled from my mouth. "Okay, I guess things are looking up a little."

Jasper stretched his arms over his head. "Some good food, a little relaxation, and tomorrow we can—"

The peal of a phone alert cut him off. Followed by a chime and a buzzing sound. And then a beep from a different direction.

All of our phones were going off.

"What the hell?" I muttered, groping for my purse.

Jasper pulled his from his pocket and stared at the screen. "Someone's asking me, 'Is this for real?' Is *what* for real?"

Quentin flicked his thumb across his screen and tapped on something. He flipped his phone sideways, squinted, and then went totally rigid in his seat. "Oh, fuck."

My gut lurched. "What is it?"

He opened his mouth and closed it again, looking too horrified to form words. All he could manage to do was beckon us over to see what had freaked him out so much.

TWENTY

Luciana

THE PHONE TREMBLED in Quentin's hand. I couldn't tell whether it was from anger, shock, or horror, because all three emotions were currently crashing through my body while I stared at the screen. I was dimly aware of Niko's phone pealing with another alert, but I couldn't tear my gaze away from the video footage playing within the frame of a public site.

Three figures moved together on a mass of rumpled bedcovers. There was Quentin, sprawled out with his head pressed into the pillow, his hips rocking. Me, bent over his thighs, my face blurred out to censor the most provocative areas while I sucked him off but identifiable in profile when I lifted my head briefly to grin at him. And Jasper, his entire hips area blurred as he pounded into me from behind.

Most of the time as we fucked each other, the average viewer probably couldn't have recognized us. The footage had been filmed from an angle that was off to the side beyond the foot of the bed. But every now and then we shifted position just enough that all of our features showed clearly.

Míerda. A shiver ran through my body, my skin chilling as if every drop of warming blood had left my veins. My legs wobbled under me, and Rafael grasped my arm to steady my balance. I barely registered the stream of curses mingling English and Spanish that flowed from his lips.

"It's already gotten more than ten thousand views," Quentin said in a hollow voice. "They're shooting up by the second."

Niko paced behind us with unusual urgency. When I managed to glance over at him, his expression was rigid. "A few major news outlets are already covering the story. They're calling it a scandal." His phone went off again, and he flinched. "Someone from the US Figure Skating organization is calling me. I've already gotten a message from the Japan Skating Federation. And several news stations."

"How the hell—how could anyone have recorded this?" I blurted out. "We were in the apartment. It was just the three of us."

Rafael's expression turned even more ominous. "Those fucking turncoats! They were taking turns guarding the apartment, remember? What day was it?"

I strained to think back through the whirl of my panicked thoughts. "The day you and Niko went to see about getting more weapons. That's why you weren't there."

Rafael balled his hands into fists. "Frankie was out there on guard duty when we left. That little prick."

Jasper blinked, looking totally dazed and a little queasy. "He snuck in and recorded us? Why the hell would he do that?"

Rafael grimaced. "The others said he's been acting off since the mall. He must have been starting to doubt whether he'd picked the right side."

The pieces clicked together in my head with sickening logic. "He was hedging his bets. Figuring if he should see if he could get anything to buy his way back into my mother's good graces if he decided to defect right back to her."

Quentin turned off his phone and then set it face down on the coffee table as if he couldn't stand to look at even the blank screen anymore. "And after you two told him off today, he did exactly that. It didn't take long for your mother to find a totally new way to attack us, huh?"

"It didn't." I swallowed hard and forced myself to check my own phone.

I had a bunch of messages popping up on my phone from unfamiliar numbers. When I opened up a couple of the social media sites and did a quick search for my skating name, a deluge of commentary on our threesome appeared. And most of it was caustic.

Slut.

Whore.

Must have slept her way into the World Championships.

I wonder how many judges she's done?

Can you imagine being that desperate?

Puking emojis. Vulgar gifs.

My blood was definitely pumping through my veins again, because my cheeks were burning with it. My stomach lurched, and I dismissed the app with a jab of my finger.

I was about to turn my phone right off when it vibrated with a notification of an incoming video chat request. An icon with Emi's picture popped up.

I hesitated, my hand tensing around the phone. Niko's sister had guessed at our joint relationship, but to have seen the proof of it in such explicit detail… I wasn't sure I wanted to face her right now.

On the other hand, she might be the only friend I had left outside this room.

Bracing myself, I hit the answer button.

Emi's face filled the whole screen, her eyes round with sympathy. "Lou, I just heard. This is crazy. Are you okay?"

How could I even answer that?

I made a vague motion with my free hand. "Not really. That video isn't something I'd ever have wanted anyone seeing. And it means one of the people we thought was an ally has betrayed us. We had no idea he even filmed us."

"I hope his ancestors rain down bad luck while they're watching over him," Emi declared with an angry huff. "I didn't watch it, of course—but people will be able to tell you didn't know you were being recorded, won't they? They'll know it's not your fault."

My mouth twisted with the misery tangling tighter inside me. "I don't know how much that'll matter. No one had any clue that I was dating Jasper *or* Quentin. For it to come out that I'm with both of them—and to come out like *this*… There are already a ton of judgmental comments all over the internet."

Emi gave me a firm look. "You're a good person, Lou. And an amazing skater. That should matter more than anything. The important people will see that."

I wished I could believe her reassurance, but it barely touched my jangling nerves. Still, I appreciated it.

"Thank you," I said. "I know you'll always see it that way. I don't suppose you have any idea how we get people focused on something else?"

Emi bit her lip. "I'm not sure. Usually it takes another big story, but you can't force that to happen." Then she brightened a bit. "But I'll think about it and let you know as soon as anything comes to me."

I had to smile at her enthusiasm, despite the nausea still churning in my gut. "That'd be great. And thank you for checking in on us too."

"Of course. Tell my brother he'd better update me as soon as he isn't so busy."

As I ended the call, I glanced over at Niko. He was still pacing while talking into his phone in brisk Japanese, sounding curter than I'd ever heard him. I'd been picking up the most useful basic phrases and bits of vocabulary here and there over the past several weeks, but I couldn't make out a single word in his rapid-fire delivery.

He ended the call and lowered his hand with a jerk. When he turned to face us, his expression was so grim it made my heart ache.

"One of our sponsors just pulled their support. I wouldn't be surprised if others do too. There are clauses in the contracts around professional conduct… I don't know how to fix this."

I rubbed my face, struggling to sort through the clash of emotions inside me. "Is there any way we could convince people that it isn't us? You can't see our faces *that* well."

Quentin frowned. "Everyone's already sure it is. Now that our names have been attached to it, I don't know how we'd change that. And it isn't like people haven't noticed the three of us skating together. If we didn't already have some connection, maybe, but…"

"Yeah." Guilt swelled up over everything else. This was my fault. "If I hadn't trusted Frankie—if my mom wasn't such a fucking *cunt*—"

Rafael slid his arm around me. "This isn't on you, Lou. You made the best decisions you could with the information you had. You three are the victims of a crime. There's nothing wrong with what you were doing."

"A whole lot of people seem to think there is." I looked desperately at Niko. "What are the skating officials saying?"

His anguished expression didn't shift. "I've only listened to a couple of the messages so far, but they're even more concerned than before about the publicity. Talking about lack of professionalism and things like that."

"Shit." Jasper raked his hand through his hair. "And the judges will hear about it—maybe even watch the recording. Even if they say it won't make them biased against us, you know it'll skew their opinions."

My agonized thoughts had already traveled even

farther than that. "Will they even allow us to compete after this kind of scandal?"

Quentin's gaze darkened. "I don't know. I don't think there's ever been a scandal quite like this in the sport."

Niko looked haunted. "I'll talk to all of them. I'll impress on them that you were the ones violated—that it was totally consensual—that it has nothing to do with your careers. And I should be able to have the video taken down… from the more legitimate sites, anyway."

His attention shot back to his phone as he got to work on a task I doubted he could have ever imagined he'd need to take on as our coach. I dropped into the nearest chair, my head spinning so fast I was dizzy and my stomach clenched tight.

Was this it? The end of everything I'd worked to achieve—destroyed because of my sex life, of all things?

Was Mom going to win after all? I could just imagine her grinning at the thought of stealing my freedom out from under me.

You might keep living, Luciana, I could hear her say, *but it won't be happily.*

I didn't want to accept that. I wanted to fight her like I had in so many ways already.

But how the hell could I turn this catastrophe around?

TWENTY-ONE

Quentin

WITH EACH SECOND THAT ticked by leading up to my cue to walk on stage, my heart thudded harder. I stared out at the set hastily assembled for this US news station's time covering the World Championships, watching the polished blond woman chatting with one of the French skaters and barely processing a single word that reached my ears.

I didn't want to be here. I wanted to give every reporter in Japan, local or otherwise, the middle finger for making such a big deal out of the leaked video.

But the controversy wasn't going away. All three of us —Lou, Jasper, and me—had gotten requests for interviews, and strangely they'd focused on me the most. Maybe they saw me as the weakest link because I wasn't actually competing. Maybe they were curious about the potential drama of my once having been Jasper's rival.

In any case, we'd decided that someone should make a public appearance to set a few things straight, and I'd rather it was me than Lou or Jasper having their focus shaken. A lot of the questions that'd started coming up were things only I could fully address anyway.

I'd taken a bullet for Lou. Handling a TV audience should be child's play.

But that didn't mean I was going to enjoy it.

There was a cut to go to commercials. One of the staff tapped my elbow. "You'll be on in a minute, Mr. Wolfe."

I nodded. The French skater had just vacated the seat next to the host's desk, where I'd be sitting in mere moments. The host sat stiffly as the makeup crew gave her face a quick touch-up.

Must be nice getting to ask all the questions and never having to be under scrutiny for anything other than your lipstick and eyeliner.

My hands twitched at my sides. I'd come alone, not wanting to expose the others to further speculation, but damn if I didn't wish I had Lou here beside me right now, smiling her fearless smile, squeezing her fingers around mine. She'd given me an emphatic kiss right before I left, and if I concentrated I could still taste her on my lips, but it wasn't the same.

I mentally smacked myself across the head. I'd survived just fine without any woman supporting me for years. I didn't *need* Lou holding my hand through this.

It just… would have been nice.

Before I could grapple with my longings any further,

the man who'd warned me motioned me out onto the stage. I plastered a tight smile on my face and strode to the waiting chair.

The glow of the studio lights glared down on me. Blinking, I settled into my seat and clasped my hands on my lap. With each passing moment, my smile felt more rigid.

"Quentin Wolfe, gold medalist in the US Junior Championships a few years back, silvers and bronzes under your belt from recent years," the host said by way of introduction. "It's an honor to have you on the show."

Somehow I didn't believe it was my medals that had her salivating to talk to me. I bobbed my head and kept that thought to myself. "I'm glad to be here, Ms. Anderson," I said, lying through my teeth.

"Oh, call me Nancy," the host said with a flash of her brilliant teeth. "You've been in the competitive figure skating circuit for quite some time, haven't you?"

They were starting with the easy questions, of course. "That's right. I registered as soon as I was old enough—made it to Nationals in my second year."

I was allowed to still be proud of the victories I'd had, wasn't I?

"Indeed you did." Nancy Anderson flashed her teeth again. "You were considered quite a promising up-and-comer with the way you burst onto the scene. How did you cope with that kind of pressure?"

I already had a standard answer to that. "Honestly, it was nothing compared to the pressure I'd always put on myself. I just saw it as extra incentive to perform my best, which I always wanted to do anyway."

Nancy tilted her head to the side with a coy expression. "It is notable that in the past year, you switched from competing in singles, as you always have in the past, to pairs during the qualifying rounds. Was there any particular reason for that?"

I shrugged as casually as I could. "I had done a little pairs skating in the past and connected with my previous partner under our coach. It seemed like a good challenge."

"And it was around that time that you met Luna Garcia."

"Yes," I said, even though it wasn't a question. After years facing my mother's demands and barrages of criticism, I knew how to keep all emotion from my face and my voice. "We were training at the same arena in Boston."

I didn't know whether to be relieved or concerned that Nancy didn't continue prodding that particular subject just yet. She leaned her chin onto her hand. "Unfortunately, it seems the switch to pairs didn't work out all that well for you. You ultimately placed too low in the Finals competition to earn a spot at the National Championships. Did you consider returning to singles?"

I kept my tone even. "It crossed my mind, but in the end that didn't work out."

Nancy raised her eyebrows. "I'm surprised by that, especially considering the intense competitive spirit you just remarked on yourself. At what point during that period did you strike up a closer relationship with Miss Garcia?"

My stomach sank with the recognition of where she was heading with the convergence of questions, but I kept my annoyance under wraps. "It wasn't until after the Finals competition. Seeing her performances made me want to get to know her better."

"Would you say your early interest in her might have been somewhat… distracting when it came to your own performance at Finals?"

There it was. She was trying to insinuate that my failures were *Lou's* fault.

How fucking dare anyone blame the woman I adored for my screw-ups.

"Not at all," I forced myself to say smoothly. "If anything, she motivated me to do my best. But it was a gamble switching to pairs so late in training, and that gamble didn't pay off. I can only blame myself for the loss."

As the words fell from my mouth and my frustration with the interview simmered inside me, it struck me for the first time how true that was. I didn't hold the slightest bit of resentment toward Jasper or any of the other skaters who'd advanced ahead of me, not anymore.

I *had* made my own choices about how to handle my career—and my personal life too. Maybe I'd started with less than other people, but I'd probably had more than some. Could I really say that my overbearing mom had been a bigger burden than Jasper's frigid asshole of a dad?

I'd carved out a spot for myself in the professional figure skating world, and I'd arrived ages ago. At this point, it really didn't matter where I'd started, did it? I had to own the decisions I'd made and the paths I'd taken rather than finding excuses for the ones that hadn't worked out.

Nancy wasn't finished speculating yet. She tapped her chin with her finger. "You could have staged a comeback at Nationals with your solo routines. Is it fair to say that your budding relationship with Ms. Garcia diverted some of your attention then?"

I couldn't completely rein in my temper, a little heat creeping into my voice. "No, I wouldn't say that's fair at all. The fact of the matter is, I wasn't able to compete in Nationals mainly because of an injury that had nothing at all to do with Lou." Okay, that was a lie, but I'd *wanted* to save her life, so fuck anyone who'd claim it was somehow her fault. "Lou has always supported my skating and encouraged me to be even better than I already am."

"Even when you were competing against each other?" Nancy asked with a light laugh that made me want to punch her carefully painted face.

I drew myself up straighter in my chair. "Yes. Even then. If anything, *I* tried to distract *her*, but she was too professional to let me get under her skin. And since I've come around to realizing that I'm better off beside her than against her, she's pushed me to up my game and encouraged me to focus on areas of my performance I'd neglected before. I'm absolutely a stronger skater because of our time together."

Nancy hesitated, as if she wasn't sure what to make of the vehemence in my voice. Then she wet her lips as if she had a particularly juicy question to come. I braced myself.

"That's wonderful to hear," she said. "But it's recently come out that your relationship with Miss Garcia is rather... unconventional. It seems she's wanted more than what you two had together."

I barely held back a snort. "If anyone had a right to be bothered by that situation, it was Jasper, not me. He and Lou were together before I even met her, and I always knew that. But something sparked between me and Lou too, and Jasper's man enough to want her to be as happy as possible more than he wants to keep her all to himself. Like they've already said in their public statements, both he and I are totally comfortable with the arrangement we have."

I wasn't going to mention there were two other men in the mix. If the media was going to find out about Niko's or Rafael's more intimate roles in Lou's life, it wouldn't be from me. They were making enough fuss over just a threesome.

Nancy nodded in a way that felt condescending. "Yes, I've heard that. It's just a little hard to believe—as I'm sure many of our viewers will agree—that such an unusual twist to your personal life wouldn't have some impact on your career."

I flexed my hands to keep them from balling into fists. This woman really didn't know how to lay a subject to rest, did she?

Well, if she needed a target other than plain old me, I could give her one.

The idea that'd just struck me sent a jolt that was both exhilaration and apprehension through my chest. For a second, my tongue turned to lead in my mouth. If I said something, if I burned that bridge so publicly—

Then what? It'd simply make it that much harder for me to go back to what I knew was an unhealthy dynamic anyway.

Lou had found the courage to speak up about what she'd endured in front of the world. And the world already had a pretty big inkling what I'd gone through. Why shouldn't I confirm it?

I fixed the host with my firmest stare. "Look, I get that the video that got out startled a lot of people. But what you all really should be worried about is catching the prick who broke into our apartment to record it. As far as my ability to skate goes, there's only one person who's ever interfered with that, and it's not Luna Garcia."

Nancy's eyes lit up with eagerness. "Care to say a little more about that, Mr. Wolfe?"

"I do." I jerked my gaze toward the cameras. "The only person who's made it harder for me to give my all on the ice is my mother. But I got tired of her beating me down and trying to control my career, and I recently cut off all ties with her. So you can expect bigger and better things from me when the next competitive circuit kicks off."

With the last announcement, a rush of relief flooded my veins. It was out in the open—I couldn't have made the separation between me and Mom more definitive.

Nancy obviously hadn't expected that declaration. Her mouth hung open for a moment before she gathered herself. "Well. That definitely sounds like it'll be exciting to see. It sounds like you're really embracing your freedom as an adult skater and this… unique relationship you've found yourself in."

"Yes," I said automatically. "I absolutely am."

My mind tripped back to my time on the rink with both Lou and Jasper. Watching them train and getting their encouragement while I worked on my own routines.

But the best had been that day when the three of us had really skated together, both of them offering me tips and demonstrating, Jasper and I passing Lou back and forth between us. More than anything that happened with us outside of our sport, right then I'd felt like I was part of something bigger than just myself. Bigger than anything I'd ever imagined was possible.

A flicker of inspiration lit in my head. I hesitated, letting it weave through my thoughts, and a smile I actually meant stretched across my face.

"You know, Nancy," I said, "I think the world should keep an eye on us. Because we might have something to show off that's a lot more worth watching than that stupid video."

Curiosity sharpened the host's eyes. "And what might that be?"

I let my smile widen. The answer would depend on how Lou and Jasper reacted to my pitch, but I was sure I could convince them one way or another. "You'll just have to wait and see."

TWENTY-TWO

Luciana

NIKO LOWERED his phone with a sigh that he quickly did his best to compensate for with a smile. I sat up on the sofa where I'd been slumped, my chest tight with trepidation. "What did they say?"

His smile tightened. "The skating officials are going to have a meeting tomorrow to make an official decision. I've reminded them as clearly as I can that the current situation isn't your fault and has nothing to do with your skating careers. If they make the right choice, they should allow you to go forward with the competition."

Jasper let out a rough sound from the chair where he was slouching and rubbed his face. "*Should* being the operative word. They're really not happy with us."

Rafael grunted from his post by the door. "You'd think

they'd appreciate the publicity you're bringing to the sport."

I grimaced. "Not this kind of publicity."

Niko wagged his finger at us. "Don't make any assumptions. We can't know what the verdict will be until they've discussed it. The facts are on your side."

The good humor in his tone didn't reach his eyes. I was sure he knew as well as I did that facts didn't mean shit in a case like this.

What mattered was that the most private details of my sex life were being shared all across the internet, and there was fuck-all I could do about it. For the rest of my life, I'd run into strangers who knew how I moved and what I sounded like in a threesome.

That wasn't the kind of fame I'd ever have wanted.

I wrapped my arm around my stomach, willing down the queasiness, and a new worry rose up. "Shouldn't Quentin be back from his interview by now?"

Jasper frowned. "It was only a half hour ago that he texted to say he was on his way back. I wouldn't call that late yet."

"I'm sure he'll be in a great mood too," I muttered sarcastically, not that I could complain when my spirits were at least as low as everyone else's in the room.

We'd come all this way. I'd worked so fucking hard. Surely all that passion and effort weren't going down the drain because of an illegal sex tape, of all things?

But I couldn't see any way out of the fate that felt more certain with every passing minute.

The lock in the apartment door clicked. I pushed to

my feet just as Quentin stepped inside, his head high and his lips curved with a... grin?

As I stared at the newest of my boyfriends, blinking in my confusion, he kicked the door shut behind him and aimed his grin at all of us while he rubbed his hands together. "I've got an idea. It might be crazy, but it could actually be perfect."

His eagerness tickled into me with a jolt of hope. "What are you talking about?"

Quentin turned to Niko rather than me. "Okabe, do you figure you're up to the challenge of throwing together a very unique routine, incredibly quickly?"

Niko took a swig from the Calpis he'd brought from the kitchen and eyed the younger man with an air of growing amusement. "I'll never refuse a challenge. But what would this routine be for?"

Quentin gestured vaguely in the air, his gaze seeking out mine and Jasper's. "I want to show the world just how well the three of us can collaborate—and that our relationship isn't something they should see as dirty. It can be art too. It's something amazing when we decide what part of it they should get to watch."

The understanding of what he was getting at seeped through my thoughts. My breath caught in my throat. "That... that could really be something." Then I paused. "You're thinking we should try to get this publicized— covered on TV and all that. Are you sure you want to make a public performance focused on the three of us?"

"Why the hell not?" Quentin demanded. "They're already making all kinds of assumptions about us based on something we wouldn't have let them see. I love you, and I love this crazy relationship we've all built together. They might as well know that on our terms rather than your mother's."

"I'm in," Jasper said, quiet but determined. "It could be a total flop—or it could blow people away. I'm willing to take that chance."

A brighter smile had crossed Niko's face. "I can already picture the routine. It'll be an honor to choreograph something like that."

My mouth opened and closed again. They were all taking a much bigger risk than I was. They were the ones with the established names that'd be tarnished if this plan only made us look ridiculous.

I wanted to try, but I didn't want to screw up their lives any more than their connection to me already had.

Before I could decide on an answer, Quentin stepped up to me and caught my hand in his. "What we've got is something special. If the world can't tell that, then they're all idiots."

His eyes gleamed with passion, and he tugged me into a kiss. The emphatic claiming of my lips melted my reservations, leaving only the glow of hope behind.

Hope and another emotion to answer the confession he'd made. When he drew back, seeking out my gaze again, I beamed up at him. "I love you too. Let's do it. Let's show them what that love really looks like."

My attention slid away from him to the other men standing around me.

Rafael with his stoic confidence and unyielding support.

Niko and his boundless serenity and warmth.

Jasper, his soulful gray-green eyes coupled with his fire-hot touch.

And Quentin in front of me, stubborn and difficult but oh-so-brilliant in ways I obviously hadn't fully appreciated yet.

My heart swelled in my chest. "I love all of you. So, so much. I think what we've built together is pretty fantastic, don't you?"

Jasper reached out to twist a strand of my hair between his fingers. A familiar light was glinting in his eyes.

He cleared his throat as a flush crept up his neck. "You know, we haven't actually *all* collaborated together. Not at the same time. That could be the perfect way to get our creativity flowing. A little inspiration?"

His tone sent a flare of heat over my skin. Looking around at the other men, I saw the same desire mirrored in all of their expressions.

I loved them, and I wanted them. I wanted to remember how wonderful this collaboration between us really was instead of getting bogged down in other people's judgments.

A little passionate fun might be just what we needed to clear our minds of all that crap and then get down to work.

I wet my lips. "I'm up for it if you all are?"

Niko's lips curved into a sly smile that left no doubt about his interest. Quentin stepped toward me, his normally cool gaze searing my skin. "Hell, yes."

Rafael's mouth twitched with what might have been a hint of a smirk. "I'll make sure the door is fully secure."

"Good thinking," I muttered.

Then Jasper tipped my chin up so he could claim a kiss, and every concern left my head except how I could enjoy even more of this delicious man.

There was a click as Rafael checked the door, and then he was behind me, his large hands sliding down my body. He eased them beneath the fabric of my leggings and tucked his fingers against the divots of my hips. With a tug to bring my ass against his groin, he showed just how much he wanted me without saying a word.

My pussy throbbed for him. But when I lifted my head, it was Quentin I saw first. He yanked off his shirt as he approached me, revealing the leanly sculpted planes of his chest. I couldn't resist tracing my fingers over the taut ridges before he grasped my tee to give me the same treatment.

As soon as he'd tossed my shirt on the ground, he gripped my ponytail and tilted my head to the side so he could nip the crook of my neck. When he flicked his tongue right up to my earlobe, trailing sparks in its wake, I couldn't restrain a gasp.

Niko tucked his head over Jasper's shoulder, his smile turning momentarily a bit shy. But after Jasper leaned into the kiss the other man offered, our coach made short work of his shirt before wrapping his arms around Jasper's waist. Watching them fall back into another kiss, long and lingering, made my pussy clench even tighter while Quentin and Rafael worked me over.

Niko turned toward me and captured my lips with his. I hummed happily against his mouth, with a sharper whimper when Quentin tweaked one nipple between his fingers.

Rafael chuckled softly. "Let me get this out of the way for you."

With a brush of his knuckles against my back, he unclasped my bra. The second the cups fell away, Quentin ducked his head to suck the peak of my breast into his mouth.

Niko drew me into another kiss and then eased back while Rafael fondled the other side of my chest from behind. As I writhed between my men, Niko tipped his head toward the bedrooms. "Should we take this to a bed? I don't know if we'll all fit on any of the ones in this apartment."

A light laugh spilled from Jasper's lips. "I think we've finally found a flaw in your country's traditions: the beds are too small."

Niko let out a playful huff. "I'm sure if we end up making a more permanent home here, we could have something custom made."

I managed to speak around another whimper. "There's plenty of room right here on the rug. I think we're good."

As if to make sure of that, Rafael stepped away from me just long enough to shove the coffee table aside. Then he spun me around and pulled me down onto the sofa, straddling his lap.

I couldn't stop myself from grinding against his rigid cock. My panties were absolutely drenched—and the situation was made even worse when Quentin came up beside us and helped Rafael strip them and my leggings right off me.

I grasped both of their flies to make sure the nakedness was kept up on all sides and glanced over my shoulder at

Jasper. "I trust you to take care of Niko. He's got *way* too many clothes on."

My partner blushed adorably but got right to work, stealing kisses from our shared boyfriend between each article he tossed aside. Then he bent over me and swept my hair to the side to nibble the corner of my jaw. "I'm not done with you yet either," he murmured in my ear.

"I'm not done with any of you, not by a long shot," I retorted, and delved my fingers inside Quentin's boxers.

His cock felt amazing, pulsing against my palm. I urged him toward me, and he knelt on the sofa, right where I could lower my head to lap my tongue over the bulging head.

As Rafael swiveled his hands against my breasts, I took Quentin all the way into my mouth. Quentin inhaled shakily and bucked to meet me, clutching at my hair again.

I felt ravenous for him, sucking harder and whirling my tongue around his length, but Quentin's grip on my hair tightened. "Slower," he rasped. "I want to enjoy every second of this."

I did as requested, my eyes finding his bright blue ones as I got back to work. His jaw clenched, his gaze burning with passion. I trailed one hand down his bare thigh where I massaged the taut muscle I found there.

When I felt his body tighten further, I pulled away. I wasn't ready for him to finish yet.

Instead, I turned back towards Rafael, moving my body in soft undulating motions against his. My hands slid across the broad expanse of his shoulders as I took in the twin burning flames that were his eyes. His kiss offered just as much fire.

I curled against him further as he bit down on my lip. With a gasp, I squirmed on his lap, desperate for release.

"You're such a brat," my bodyguard crooned. "You know how to make me want you so fucking badly. God, I want to take you right here, right now."

I dipped my head toward his. "So what's stopping you?" I whispered.

Something primal clicked inside of him. He picked me up while I giggled breathlessly in his arms and laid me flat on the rug. The head of his cock pressed between my folds. My lips parted in a gasp, but it was smothered by another kiss.

Somewhere in there, a foil packet ripped. Before I could register what was happening, Rafael pressed forward inside of me. I groaned, my eyelids fluttering closed. The sensation of him filling me up felt so right.

He thrust forward slowly, teasing me with his length, and then, all of a sudden, he pulled out. I whimpered in disappointment, but that only put a smile on his face.

"If you want more, you're going to have to work for it. Let's see what you can do. Get Jasper and Niko off at the same time, and then I'll let you have what you want."

Challenge accepted.

I shot him a teasing grin, and then eased off him to scoot towards my next two targets. They were willing victims; both Jasper and Niko were rock hard before I even got my hands on them.

They eased to the floor on either side of me. I kissed Jasper hard and then claimed Niko's mouth, tasting their flavors mingled together on each other's lips to thrilling effect. My hands raked thin red lines down their bodies as they swayed toward me.

Their warmth was enough to melt away all my previous worries. Every ounce of anxiety that had previously taken up space inside my head and heart evaporated into the atmosphere, leaving me with nothing but their protective, hungry love.

Still passing kisses back and forth, I reached out with both hands and grasped their untended erections. Their matching groans made a perfect symphony. Simultaneously, I ran my thumbs over the head of their cocks. Niko's teeth nicked my lower lip in the middle of our kiss, and Jasper thrust into my grasp.

"God, Lou," he groaned, "you can't just tease me like this."

Niko's hips jerked upward. "Right. That's my job."

I smirked at the sight. They were fully under my control—but that didn't mean that I would keep it for long. Jasper was gasping, but he was quickly gaining a handle on himself. As he rocked into my hand, he tilted my chin up to look at him.

The firestorm in his eyes sparked up a river of desire within my core. My legs shifted together, my pussy clenching in my center. I was desperate for satisfaction. Teasing Niko and Jasper was getting me hotter than I could stand.

As if sensing my need, Niko reached between my legs. He fingered my clit with the same eager energy he brought to so much else, setting of a flood of starker pleasure through my nerves. My knees wobbled. When he hooked one finger right inside me, I outright moaned.

Apparently Rafael needed satisfaction too. The next thing I knew, he was crouching on the floor behind me, his breath spilling hot down my spine.

"You did a good enough job," he growled. "I guess you deserve a little bit of a reward."

"I do," I gasped, writhing between the three of them. "I really do."

He wasn't stingy with rewarding me. His hands traveled around my body, leaving a scorching trail of bliss wherever they touched. My lips parted with a feverish panting. I allowed the pleasure to take over, to become my sole focus.

Quentin's cocky voice broke through my reverie. "Don't forget to share."

He'd hunkered down on the floor too. Before I could figure out exactly how to attend to him too, Rafael took over for me.

"Suit yourself up and get over here," he growled at the younger man.

As Quentin grabbed another condom, Niko and Jasper eased a little apart. I let go of them for just long enough for Rafael to lift me off the floor—to make room for Quentin to slide beneath me. He slid one hand down to adjust his pulsing member, inviting me to sheath myself on it.

I didn't deny him. The feeling of him sliding into me felt like fireworks in my core. I rocked my hips against him, keeping Rafael in my peripheral vision as he positioned himself behind me. When the bigger man nudged his erection against my back opening, I nodded in eager anticipation and leaned forward to allow him easier entrance.

His thick cock felt like fire at first, but after his first few strokes, nothing but ecstasy raced through my veins. The two of them filling me together felt like heaven. With every joint thrust, I was soaring higher.

"God, don't stop," I moaned, not even knowing which of them I was referring to. Both, really. "Please don't."

But I couldn't neglect my other two men, even if Rafael had decided I'd completed my duty. Through the haze of pleasure, I swayed to the side and hovered my mouth over Niko's straining cock.

"You're amazing, Angel," he murmured as he adjusted his position to allow me better access.

I caught Jasper's gaze and jerked my head toward our coach. "Let's make sure Niko has *all* the inspiration he needs."

Lust flared in Jasper's eyes. As I sucked Niko down, he positioned himself behind the other man. Careful of the still healing injury on Niko's chest, he tucked his arm around Niko's slim waist. The giddy shudder of Niko's body against mine told me when Jasper had slid inside him.

I took that as a cue to up my pace. I took all of him, as much as I was able to. It was all I could do to keep my mouth bobbing up and down over his musky skin while Quentin and Rafael send more bliss spiraling through me with their increasingly frantic rhythm. Every part of me was filled, but it wasn't just my pussy that felt close to bursting. Love and awe resonated through my chest.

As I careened toward the edge, Quentin gave a sharper jerk upward. He let out a ragged sound as he came. With him still inside me, I pressed back into Rafael's thrusts—and he flung me even higher with one final plunge of his cock. His strangled breath told me he'd joined me.

I moaned my climax around Niko's cock. As Rafael spilled himself, I stroked Niko's balls. He rocked between me and Jasper for a few more seconds before spurting his release into my mouth.

"Fuck," Jasper groaned from behind him. He bit down on Niko's shoulder as he joined our mass coming. Then, as I lifted my head, he leaned across the other man to claim one last kiss from me.

I rolled off Quentin to collapse between my men, my chest heaving, every part of me alight with the afterglow. The four of them cuddled closer, each finding some part of my naked, sweat-damp body to caress.

"Wow," Jasper said with a hoarse laugh. "We really pulled that off. What would you call it—a five-some?"

A giggle spilled out of me. Every shred of anxiety had left my body with that epic collision of passion. "That sounds about right."

Niko's eyes twinkled. "Don't doubt what we can accomplish when we work together."

A grin stretched my lips. Yes. We were capable of just about anything.

I tapped him on the chest. "Which means we can pull off Quentin's crazy plan too. So you'd better get started choreographing."

TWENTY-THREE

Luciana

A HANDFUL of the media channels we'd invited out to the arena were already there before we'd even arrived. More trickled in as we put on our skates and went through our warm-up. By the time we were ready for the actual performance, we had a whole row of reporters waiting for whatever we had to show them, the cameras in their midst blinking little red lights.

As I took my position between Jasper and Quentin, my chest tightened. I had to make a conscious effort to loosen my lungs with deep breaths. It was way too late to turn back now. We'd either pull this thing off or make total fools of ourselves, only compounding the disgrace we were in with the skating community.

Dios mío, let it be the first option.

I stared down at the ice for a moment as if I could see

right through it. We'd only had a matter of hours to practice the hastily choreographed routine, not weeks or even months like we normally would have.

But Niko had made it as easy as possible on us by using moves from our existing routines in similar arrangements, just figuring out simple ways to expand and combine those elements—ways that were more about artistry than complex physical stunts. I *knew* we could handle every part of it.

We had to show the world the real beauty of our collaboration.

Jasper glanced over at me. His sea-green costume both contrasted with and complimented the flame-red one Quentin had on and my own pearly pale get-up. Since we didn't have matching costumes for all three of us, we'd gone with an array instead, and Niko had taken that visual aspect into account with the choreography.

"Are you all right?" my partner asked.

I shot him a quick smile. "Yeah. Nervous, but we've got this, right?"

The corner of Jasper's mouth curled upward. "You bet we do. This'll be a heck of a lot easier than some of the moves we've pulled off in the past."

I couldn't help laughing at the truth of his statement. "No kidding."

Quentin rolled his shoulders. "We'll go out there and skate and then head home. Let the reporters and the skating officials make whatever they want of it. After we do our bit, it's not up to us anymore."

I exhaled in a rush. "Sounds good to me."

If Jasper could smile through this—grumpy Jasper

who had once scowled through a week's worth of practices —then couldn't I? If Quentin, the cocky asshole of the year, could come up with an idea that could bring us all together, how could I do anything other than believe in it?

I squared my shoulders. For them, I would fly to the moon just to snatch them a handful of stars.

Niko motioned to us from the stands, where he had the music ready to play. He was beaming as cheerfully as ever, but I could tell the crowd of reporters was getting antsy.

I nodded, and the three of us shifted into our opening poses. My blood pounded through my veins, but I let the rhythm lift my spirits rather than rattling them.

Just make it through this, and then we can go home. Just believe in the plan. Believe in the men who've stood by me through so much.

The song started to drift through the PA system. With the opening notes, the crowd of onlookers melted from my mind. All that was left was Quentin and Jasper, and the knowledge that Niko and Rafael were watching from the benches, full of love and support.

I allowed myself to be taken in by the gentle melody as I drifted gracefully across the ice. Between my two lovers, I could imagine that I floated in a soft bubble of protection that was much more tender than the world outside.

It was a short routine, about the length of a typical short program, but we were making the most of it—and of our trio. I spun from Quentin to Jasper and back again. Their hands lingered on my sides, my shoulders, love glowing in their eyes.

We pulled off a triple Salchow in perfect sync, three

blades clacking against the ice with our landing in time with the music. My men whipped around me and grasped me on either side.

This was one of the trickier parts of the routine, but we'd kept the lift itself simple, knowing that having two men as the base would be a spectacle in itself. Quentin and Jasper hoisted me into the air by my calves and then my feet, holding me above their shoulders as we glided forward. I arced my arms gracefully through the air.

As they lowered me, I risked a glance at the audience. Everyone's eyes were glued to us, still and silent as they took in our performance.

Was that awe on their faces or doubt? Quentin swirled me around and sent me careening toward Jasper, and for a second, I lost track of my feet. I reached Jasper at a slightly wrong angle, off-balance for the spin we were meant to complete.

I wobbled—and Jasper's strong arms managed to right me. He swung me around, and my body loosened again as I felt it lock into the right position.

It didn't matter what the spectators thought. *We* knew that what we could make together was beautiful. If they couldn't see it, it was their loss.

We pranced across the ice in a swift sequence of footwork. I caught a brief sway from Quentin, who'd stretched himself the most to learn this specific section of the routine, but he caught himself so quickly I wasn't sure the audience would even have noticed.

We were moving in harmony, totally aware of each other's presence, totally united in our love and our passion for our art.

The music swelled and so did my pride. Quentin glided up at my left side, Jasper on my right. We were in the home stretch—just a few epic moves to end things with a smash. Well, hopefully not a literal one.

I gave myself over to the second lift, letting Quentin grip my shoulder while Jasper swept my hips into the air. We spiraled around as one being, my arm and leg lifting to add elegance to the pose.

Then, with the cue in the music, the two men pushed themselves faster. They launched me into the air so I could spin with a graceful double toe-loop jump. I could have tried for a triple, but we'd felt that would be too risky with the unusual launch.

Almost there. I wove between Jasper and Quentin, forming an infinity symbol with my path as we skated forward, and then fell back into synchronization with them. As much as I wanted to look into their faces and draw confidence from them, I had to focus on my own portion of this next move.

At the trill in the song, we all pushed off into our triple Axels. My legs whipped off the ice, my hands outstretched towards the stands. I was defying gravity, flying high, and connecting with the ice in a stable landing that reverberated through my lowered leg.

Next to me, Jasper's leg dipped to catch his balance. Not an absolutely perfect landing, but it was impressive that we'd pulled off the synchronized jump at all with so little practice. He regained his form in an instant.

We whirled together in a three-part spin that Niko had invented specifically for this routine. My heart soared as I leaned back with one hand extended. Watching this moment from the videos Niko had recorded had taken my breath away. I could only hope it was doing the same for our audience now.

But if it didn't, I still knew the three of us were creating something marvelous, something bigger than we were as individuals. If the rest of the world couldn't see that, there was nothing else left that we could show them.

The whirlwind that kept me in motion slowed, and we twined our arms in an ending pose that spoke of solidarity and devotion, our heads dipped together. My breath was coming hard, and I could hear the guys panting, but there was elation in the sound.

We'd completed the whole routine with no major mistakes. We'd offered up a performance like nothing the professional skating world had accepted before.

Now all that was left was the audience's reaction.

In the first few seconds after the music faded out, there was total silence. My pulse gave a nervous hiccup.

Then applause rang out from the stands, along with a couple of eager whoops.

A smile sprang to my face. We turned and bowed together with clasped hands while the clapping continued. A sense of resolve glowed in my chest.

Even if this performance wasn't enough to prove that we were more than a salacious news story and that our joint relationship was nothing to be ashamed of, it should have been. We knew what we stood for.

Now everything depended on just how closed-minded the skating officials decided to be.

TWENTY-FOUR

Luciana

VOICES RESONATED all around me beneath the rink's high ceiling. Jasper, Quentin, and I had been ambushed by reporters the second we'd stepped off the ice. They seemed to be running some kind of rotation, talking to each of us.

Thankfully, so far everyone had sounded upbeat and even excited about the performance. The man aiming his microphone at my face right now was grinning. "Finally, I have to ask: what prompted the three of you to pull together this unexpected routine?"

I had to laugh. "I think that should be pretty obvious. There's been a lot of talk about us in the news lately, and we wanted to show another side to the story."

As the man nodded and made a few concluding remarks to the camera, Niko leaned his head over from behind me. "The comments on the live broadcasts are blowing up," he said under his breath. "It's all been really positive. The fans are loving the performance—and all three of you."

A smile sprang to my lips, just in time for another reporter to dart into the gap in front of me. She pointed her mic toward me, her eyes shining.

"Luna Garcia, it's great to speak with you today. What were you hoping to get across with this routine?"

The answer came easily. "All three of us wanted to show the skating world that there's nothing wrong with us being together—in whatever way we'd like to be—and that we can create something amazing in collaboration."

She rattled off a couple more questions. After I'd answered, she lowered the mic, her voice dropping to a hush.

"You know, I've always wondered if it wouldn't be good to allow pairs skating with two women or two men and see how *that* would work out. It was thrilling to watch what you put together here—it makes me think there could be so many other possibilities."

My smile widened. "I'd love to see more variety in pairs too. Everything doesn't have to be so… so cookie-cutter standard to be beautiful."

"I agree." She lifted the mic back to her lips and glanced at the camera held behind her. "Well, there you have it, everyone—a statement from the woman herself. We can't ask for anything more than that…"

As she turned away, a deep sigh escaped me. Slowly, we were making the world see what we could do. It might take a lot of time and a metric fuck-ton of work, but they *would* accept us.

I was glad for the enthusiastic response, but we weren't in the clear yet. If the skating officials weren't convinced, we might still be banned from Worlds.

I glanced around at the crowd, bracing myself for another round of questioning, but instead my gaze caught on a figure bursting past the door at the back of the stands. Ursula hurtled down the steps with her straggly blond hair flying behind her, only slowing when she noticed the milling group of reporters around us.

At the sight of the tension gripping her face, my stomach flipped over. I ducked behind Quentin and hustled over to the steps. Ursula dashed down to meet me a little apart from the crowd.

"What are you doing here?" I murmured urgently.

She made a face. "I tried to text and call you, but you weren't replying. I didn't think this was news that could wait."

I winced. I'd left my phone in my purse—and on vibrate—while we warmed up and hadn't checked it since. It wasn't as if I had a pocket to keep it on me when I was in my skating costume.

"Sorry. What's going on?"

Ursula flicked her gaze toward the reporters and dropped her voice even lower. "Your mom just arrived in Tokyo with a bunch of her people. What I'm hearing is that she's determined to take you out of the equation once and for all, and to do it herself—she's pissed about the 'spectacle' you've made of the family or something like that. It sounds like she's gone even more off the rails than before."

My heart plummeted with a sudden desperate chill. Mom was right here in this city—and out for my blood? We'd just publicized our location all over the news.

We had to get out of here.

Niko sidled over to join us, his expression darkening as he took in my own. "What's the matter, Angel?"

I swallowed thickly. "We've got to leave—fast. My mom could be on her way to start a bloodbath right now. Can you give the reporters some kind of excuse to explain why we need to head out?"

Niko's eyes widened. "Not a problem. Leave it to me."

He strode back to the crowd and said a couple of brisk sentences in Japanese, followed by an English translation: "We appreciate that you've spent this time with us today, but my skaters have an important appointment to get to. We look forward to talking to you more after their next performance!"

As the reporters started to file out, I hurried over to take off my skates and grab my bag. Jasper took in my face and clenched his jaw. "That bad, huh?"

I nodded. "We have to head out as quickly as possible. And find someplace to strategize that we're absolutely sure my mom couldn't know about."

Niko hefted his own bag. "I can think of a spot where no one is likely to be looking for a group of skaters. Are we taking Ursula and Dámaso with us?"

"Yeah. Text the directions to Ursula so they can follow us."

We marched up the steps and out to our SUV. Rafael

fell into step with me halfway across the parking lot. I shot him a look and simply said, "My mom's here."

From the twitch of his expression, I could tell he understood just how dire our situation was.

I scanned the parking lot before leaping inside, relieved to see no sign of Mom's presence yet. For all I knew, she was still at the airport going through customs.

But she wouldn't stay there for long.

As Niko hit the gas, Quentin gazed at the streets beyond the SUV's windows, his face paler than usual. "Do you really think she'll be able to figure out where our new apartment is? We just moved there."

I shook my head. "I doubt it. But I think we should take every precaution just in case. We don't know all the resources she might have in this country."

Niko drove through the city with focused intensity and pulled the car into a parking garage. We followed him out onto the sidewalk, where Ursula and Dámaso caught up with us, and up to a building with neon signs glowing in the windows and vibrant paint splashed across the building's face.

"This is a love hotel," Niko said as he motioned us to the front door. "We don't need ID, and we can pay by the hour. No way for anyone to know we're here unless they spot us going in."

I couldn't restrain a hitch of a laugh. "Imagine how much trouble we'll be in with the figure skating organizations if they get wind of this hang-out."

His logic made sense, though. We let Niko handle the room selection and payment, and within a matter of minutes, we were filing into a large hotel room with an obvious rose theme. There were fake roses smothering the walls, rose-print sheets and duvet, roses in a vase on the side table, and a thick rose scent clogging the air.

Dámaso sneezed. "This is… This is really something."

"It is," Niko said, chipper as ever, but his eyes had darkened. "I suppose we need to decide what we're doing next?"

I turned to the turncoats. "Have you heard anything else from your contacts who are still working with my mom?"

Dámaso waggled his phone. "It sounds like she got to the arena just a few minutes ago. We left right in time."

Ursula shuddered. "She's going to be hunting the city for us—me and Dámaso as well as the five of you."

"Has there been any word from Frankie?" I asked, holding on to the tiniest shred of hope that maybe he could change sides again and give us an inside advantage.

Ursula grimaced. "Nothing at all from that jackass."

"Okay." I clasped my hands in front of me and paced from the bed to the wall and back again. "We can't keep practicing while my mom is looking for us. It'll be too easy for her to find us that way."

Jasper frowned. "If you're going to suggest we give up on Worlds after everything—"

I held up my hand. "No. I'm just talking through our options." I heaved a ragged breath. "We could notify the police and hope they round her up—or at least her people—but she probably wouldn't risk coming here unless she or an ally in the Devil's Dozen has at least a few officers on their payroll, so that tactic might not work out in our favor after all. And even if not, it wouldn't be that hard for her to avoid them while she searches for me."

Rafael tipped his head to the side. "Didn't the Storm say he'd send people to help if we needed it?"

"Yeah. But I don't know how they'll find Mom and her people to take them out either. She'll know he's on my side by now—she's probably going to avoid any of the Devil's Dozen's usual haunts." My stomach knotted. "Her whole focus is destroying me."

"So far none of these options sound very good," Niko said gently.

"I know." I rubbed my forehead. The truth of the situation was creeping up on me; I just didn't want to accept it.

But there was no getting around it. Mom had forced my hand. I couldn't simply lay low and dodge her attacks.

It wasn't just my life on the line but my men's and my loyal allies' too.

I dragged in a breath. "I can't keep running away from her and pretending my family legacy doesn't exist. Worlds is coming up fast. Even if there was a way to practice in secret, we couldn't risk showing up at the competition if she might come and open fire on all those people. She's already shown she doesn't care about killing innocent kids to punish me."

Rafael was watching me, his mouth set at an even grimmer angle than usual. "Where are you going with this, Lou?"

I raised my head and met his eyes. "We have to end this conflict completely. I have to face her head on and make sure she'll never be a problem again."

A momentary silence fell over the room. Ursula cleared her throat. "You mean kill her."

Nausea swept through my gut, but I couldn't deny it. "I wanted to be done with the violence, but she keeps flinging more at me. The longer I've avoided that one step, the worse things she's done. It's time—and then maybe I really can leave the rest behind for good."

Quentin grasped my arm and gave it a reassuring squeeze. "If you decide you'd rather just take off and forget about Worlds, I don't think any of us will argue with you. We're sticking with you no matter what."

A lump rose in my throat. "Thank you. You have no idea how much that means to me. But no matter where I go, she's going to keep tracking me down. I can't live like that."

Jasper inclined his head. "Then you've got to do what you've got to do. None of us will judge you for taking that step either. I know this isn't how you'd have wanted to handle the problem."

"That's right," Niko said firmly. "Whatever you decide, we'll stand with you and do whatever we can to help. It won't change—"

The peal of his phone's ringtone cut him off. He fished his phone out of his pocket and glanced at the screen. His eyebrows leapt up.

"It's one of the skating officials I've been talking with. I'd better take this."

He took a few steps away and launched into a conversation in brisk but cheery Japanese. I couldn't understand a word of it, but that didn't stop me from trying to read his body language.

Of course, Niko was always so animated it was hard to guess how the discussion was going. I watched as his shoulders sank and then perked up again. His hand waved in the air even though the person on the other end couldn't see his gestures. I couldn't tell whether he was putting a good face on horrible news or happily accepting welcome news.

My heart drummed in a heavy rhythm. By the time Niko finished the call and turned back to us, my mouth had gone completely dry. Even with the threat of wholesale slaughter hanging over me and the people I cared about most, I needed to know the verdict.

Niko's broad grin soothed my nerves in the instant before he spoke. "We did it! The consensus is that you should be allowed to compete—and that's their formal position going forward. They are considering you to be on probation, but as long as no new sex tapes start circulating, I think we'll be okay."

Jasper's eyes lit up. "That's fantastic!"

The rush of joyful relief washed through me and seemed to leave me feeling hollowed out. We'd succeeded, we'd proved our point—but I couldn't fully enjoy that fact while my head remained on my mother's chopping block.

"It is great," I said. "Now we need to make sure we can actually show up at Worlds without it turning into a mass murder scene."

Rafael stepped closer to me, but even his looming presence wasn't as comforting as usual. "I can handle your mother if you want. You just say the word, and you won't have to be involved at all. I don't want you to get your hands dirty if it's going to weigh on your conscience."

I smiled up at him, my heart swelling with love. It didn't surprise me that he'd make the offer, but it meant a lot that he had all the same.

"Thank you," I said. "But I don't think sending you to take her out would make me feel better. You'd still be acting on my orders. I'd feel even more guilty sending you into the danger alone."

He let out a scoffing sound. "I can deal with that."

I grasped his hand. "I know you can. But it still doesn't feel right." I shook myself, trying to work the tension out of my nerves. "Anyway, I have an even bigger problem than that. Once Mom is gone, the Devil's Dozen members are going to expect me to step up and take her place. Even if you're willing to take *that* role, I'm not sure they'll just take my word that you're qualified for the job."

Quentin rubbed his mouth. "So we don't only need to figure out how to off your mom but also how to handle what'll happen right after. Rafael killing her wouldn't be enough?"

"Not if he kills her as my bodyguard, protecting me." I let out a groan. "Why did I have to be born a Cordova?"

But I had been, and there'd been privileges to my life as well as downsides. Who knew how I'd have turned out in some other family? Maybe I'd never have found skating at all or never had the means to pursue it.

Speculating didn't get me anywhere. The fact was, as long as my mom was living, I could never be free. And as long as there was no one else to inherit the Deadly Rose throne, I could never live how I wanted to, even though I couldn't be less interested in the job. If only—

An idea struck me like a bolt of lightning. I had to

pause and catch my breath as it unfurled through my mind. A giddy shiver ran through my chest.

I looked up into Rafael's dark eyes again. "I might know how to pull this off. But I'm going to need your help."

He didn't hesitate for even an instant with his response. "Whatever you need, it's already yours."

"Good. I'm going to arrange a meeting with my mom tomorrow."

TWENTY-FIVE

Luciana

I BREATHED in the dusty air with its scent of old, varnished wood and willed my nerves to settle. Not that I could actually feel calm, but I'd rather not be totally jittery if I could help it.

The theater that'd been out of use for a few years seemed like the perfect setting for this confrontation. I stood with Quentin, Jasper, and a few dozen figures that Beckett and the Blood Hunter had sent to support me off in the wings on one side of the stage, the curtains rippling around me. No one else was around—no unwitting citizens who could get caught in the crossfire.

Mom wasn't going to distract me that way. This one thing, we were doing on my terms.

I hadn't spoken to her directly. Ursula had ensured the message trickled through her contacts to my mother, and we'd gotten confirmation that the Deadly Rose had agreed to a parlay here just this morning. But I could easily imagine Mom's face hardening as she heard the request.

I could imagine her spitting her agreement into my face. *We can do this wherever you want, Luciana. Pick where you want to die, because that's all you'll get from me now.*

My heart thudding, I waited for her to arrive. My fingers curled around my pistol. I touched my knife in its sheath at my hip just to reassure myself of its presence.

Jasper and Quentin adjusted their own grips on their guns, scanning the rows of seats beyond the stage. We'd left Niko tucked away in the rosy love hotel room, because I'd insisted I wasn't putting him through physical combat while he was still recovering from the last time my mother's people had shot him. But he'd helped in his own ways.

All of the Devil's Dozen lackeys who'd joined us were armed and ready as well. Ursula and Dámaso crouched near the back of the stage, their gazes flicking over the theater. Beckett's and the Blood Hunter's people were clearly disciplined and focused. Not a murmur escaped them or a restless stirring passed through their cluster—a few in front of me as a shield and the others gathered behind me—as the seconds ticked down to my mother's entrance.

The door we'd left unlocked creaked open at the far end of the building. I made out the faint scuffing of various footsteps. My shoulders tensed, and my gun-hand bobbed up a few inches.

The curtains at the other end of the stage swayed. My mother stepped forward, surrounded by a mass of lackeys.

She had to have brought at least as many people as I had around me. But that wouldn't matter in the end.

She peered between the two men standing guard in front of her with an expression as icy as I'd pictured. Her voice came out equally cold. "So you're willing to look me in the face after you stabbed me in the back. I'm surprised you didn't flee the country the instant you heard I was on my way."

My heart thumped so hard I'd swear I felt my ribs rattle, but I raised my chin, refusing to let my anxiety show. "I'm not backing down. I'm claiming my life to live it the way I want. And I didn't stab you in the back. You attacked me first, more than once. All I did was defend myself and the people I care about the only way I could."

Her lips curled with disdain. Spittle flecked the air as she hurled her next words at me. "So caught up in your silly little competitions. My daughter, prancing around on the ice. But you're not my daughter anymore. No daughter of mine would have made a mockery of our name and dragged me through the mud!"

A prickle of rage sparked inside me along with a tremor of confusion. "How did I drag you through the mud or anything else? I'm not even competing using my actual last name! No one has any idea that you have anything to do with Luna Garcia—or, at least, they'd never have known anything about my mother if you hadn't kept lashing out. You should have let me go quietly."

Mom jabbed her finger at me. "No. You belong to me. You're mine, Luciana, and you don't get to just wander off. After all the time I spent preparing you—everything I invested in you—this is how it's supposed to be. You're not allowed to walk away."

She was really raving now. Did her underlings hear how unhinged she sounded?

"I didn't ask for any of that," I retorted. "And I've invested *my* time in the things I care about—skating and people who support me in my dream. You could have chosen anyone else out of all the people who actually want the job to be your heir."

"That's not how this works! You're a Cordova—you're the heir to the Deadly Rose. I shouldn't have to settle for some pendejo off the street. But you're too stupid to see that. I never should have let you get wrapped up in skating in the first place. It's warped your brain."

I couldn't restrain a snort even as my hackles rose at her insults. "The only warped brain around here is yours. You sound like a lunatic. Why would I have wanted to stay with you, to keep learning the things you wanted me to learn? I chose my path, and you've turned it into a shitshow, not me."

She bared her teeth at me. "I won't take the blame for this. You and everyone you roped into your pointless dream are going to pay for it *today*. Or did you think you could beg for mercy?"

There was my perfect opening. I squared my shoulders, ignoring the chalkiness of my mouth and the thunder of my pulse, and took a step forward.

Quentin and Jasper stirred uneasily as I moved away from them, but they didn't stop me. They knew this part of the plan, as much as they'd hated it.

The men who'd shielded me parted to let me through.

I took another steady step forward onto the stage, holding my mother's gaze. Then another, and another.

A nervous quiver ran down my spine. With every additional distance I put between myself and my supporters, I felt increasingly naked. But we weren't going to get anywhere I needed to go unless I put myself on the line like this.

Mom stared at me, her eyes narrowing as if expecting this move to be some kind of trick. Which maybe it was, but it didn't have to be. I was giving her one more chance to do right by me, to let it simply be over.

Not that I had any real hope she'd take that chance.

When I reached the middle of the stage, where a pool of starker spotlight fell across the polished boards, I stopped. As I held Mom's gaze, I lifted my voice to carry through the large room.

"Mom, this is your last chance to listen to me. The Deadly Rose was always a role you were trying to force me into, not something I wanted. I'd have been pretending the whole time, not really living, because it isn't what I'm meant to do. Ruling through terror, dealing out violence —it makes me sick to my stomach. It always did. That's just who I am; I can't help it."

I tossed my gun off the side of the stage, letting it land amid the empty seats, well beyond reach. Then I unsheathed my knife and chucked it in the same direction, leaving me totally unarmed. If I'd felt naked before, now I might as well have been bared to the bone.

Mom's lips parted with the slightest hint of shock.

I didn't let my gaze waver. "I'm making my stand. I don't want any more blood on my hands. You can accept who I am and let go of this idea that you have to use me as a puppet, or you can do whatever else you want to with me. How we end this stand-off is up to you."

I held my arms out, offering myself up as I was.

Mom's eyes burned into mine, those two dark brown orbs that were so like my own. Her jaw worked. She might even have considered going with the first option I'd given her.

But if she did, it was only for a second before the sneer crossed her lips again. She lifted her head at a haughty angle and let out a bitter laugh.

Then she twitched her gun where she held it by her thigh. "A disappointment right until the end. At least you've made this final moment as easy for me as it could possibly be. I'll take care of the problem I raised myself."

She jerked her hand toward her men. "Make sure we're not interrupted."

At her gesture, the men around her surged forward—past me, to stand between us and my allies so no one could rush to my aid. Mom stalked forward in their wake, her fingers tightening around her gun. My body shook with the drumming of my heartbeat, but I held myself still and firm, while every nerve screamed at me to run.

Mom halted just a couple of steps away. She started to raise her pistol to point it at me, probably planning to shoot the bullet right through the middle of my forehead.

But she didn't get that far.

With a swift hiss, a figure plunged down from above. Rafael plummeted toward my mother, fixed to a cable like the kind I'd used when practicing the hardest figure skating jumps and lifts for the first time.

It worked just as Niko and the two men who'd helped him set it up had promised. My bodyguard soared through the air, dropping straight to the stage in the space of a blink.

Mom didn't even have time to glance up before he'd rammed the heavy knife he was holding right into the top of her skull.

A croaking sound escaped Mom's throat as her eyes fogged over. She crumpled to the floor of the stage. Her limbs shuddered and sagged. Blood pooled through the scattered strands of her dark hair.

Rafael stepped between me and her as if to protect me from the sight. As if I didn't need with every fiber of my being to be sure she was truly gone.

My stomach churned, but I held steady. With the image of Mom's death burned behind my eyes, I swiveled around to face the not-quite-empty rows of seats.

"My mother is dead," I declared, heaving my voice out into the room. Then I spun to face the gaping underlings poised between me and my supporters. "The old Deadly Rose is gone, which means you answer to me now. I won't have you hurting me or my people."

The goons hesitated in their bewilderment, not knowing what orders to follow when the woman who'd given their previous ones was dead. As they wavered, my allies charged into their midst, knocking guns from hands and slamming anyone who resisted against the floorboards.

In the time it took me to heave a few breaths, Mom's entire force was subdued—and now looking both confused and disgruntled. They stared at me as if waiting for further direction.

They were looking at the wrong person.

I swept my hand toward Rafael, who still had the bloody knife clutched in his large hand. "As the new Deadly Rose, my first act is to hand over the title and leadership over the Cordova empire to Rafael Torres. From now on, you answer to him. He's clearly proven he's up to the task."

The thugs' gazes darted between me and my former bodyguard, and I thought I saw respect starting to light in a few pairs of eyes. But they weren't the only ones I was speaking to.

I swung back toward the seemingly absent audience and projected my voice even louder. "Can everyone accept that, or do we have any questions?"

Along the railing of the balcony that jutted out over half of the lower seats, twelve figures stepped from the shadows into view. I immediately made out Beckett's confident stance and the Blood Hunter's watchful face. The reps I'd met for the March Wind and the Bright Dragon held up phones streaming video chats so that their bosses could take in the confrontation and its result from afar.

Most of the other eight spectators were reps as well, holding their own phones to send these events back to the Devil's Dozen bigwigs they stood for. A couple of the others, older men with stern faces, looked over the stage with their hands resting on the railing. Members who'd come to see these events in person, I guessed, though I didn't know what names they went by.

One way or another, every existing member of the Devil's Dozen had witnessed the death of the Deadly Rose. Everyone had seen Rafael take her life in spectacular fashion.

I'd needed them to not just see her gone, but also have it burned into their minds just how powerful the man beside me could be.

Beckett raised his voice first, with a subtle nod toward me. "I accept Rafael Torres as the new Deadly Rose. I welcome him into the Devil's Dozen as an equal and a colleague."

"I accept him too," the Blood Hunter announced, more bluntly. "Good to have you with us, Rafael."

Their voices started a cascade. One and then another face on the phone's screens spoke, and their reps confirmed their acknowledgment of Rafael's new position. The two other members who'd come in person hesitated the longest, but finally bowed their heads and added their agreement.

Even as relief washed over me, my stomach didn't completely unknot. The rest of the Devil's Dozen would be keeping a close eye on Rafael, no doubt, watching for any sign of weakness. Maybe even hoping for a chance to get the better of him.

I suspected their quick acceptance of my choice was partly because they hadn't wanted *me* to take my mother's place anyway. It had to be obvious to everyone other than her how bad I'd be at that job.

But I was okay with that. And I knew Rafael *was* up to the task.

Anyone who tried to take him down would quickly regret it.

Rafael's new band of underlings had crowded around him, professing their loyalty. This political segment of his life was novel to him, but I had all the faith in the world in him, just like he'd had in me for these past ten years.

My gaze dropped to my mother's discarded body, still lying center stage in a widening puddle of blood. Taking in her contorted features and the sharp angles of her strewn limbs, a pang of sadness hit me.

I wouldn't miss her. Every day from now on, I'd feel nothing but gratitude for the fact that she was no longer in my life. But I couldn't help wishing I could have had a different mother—a kinder one, a loving one who'd at least tried to understand me.

But it said everything anyone needed to know about what kind of woman Mireya Cordova was, that when faced with her daughter helpless and asking for peace, she'd instead come at me with a weapon and every intention of murdering me.

Now the monster she'd proved herself to be was gone. A new legacy could begin, one I wouldn't really be a part of.

Which was just fine with me. I had a different legacy to carve out for myself, one I could now pursue unhindered.

TWENTY-SIX

Jasper

IF YOU ASKED me what was worse, the war with Lou's mom and her goons or the challenge of facing the skating officials, judges, and immense audience at the World Championships today, I'd have had a little trouble answering. Okay, having guns pointed at me and fearing for Lou's life—and my own—was a nightmare. But I'd had plenty of nightmares about competitions like the one we were about to complete too.

Lou nudged me as our paths crossed during the group warm-up before the free skate routines started. "Don't look so grim. We've got this."

Her bright smile lifted my spirits, along with the memory of our last few practices, when we'd finally pulled off our new transition perfectly. Only a couple of times, and we'd still been shaky during the last practice, so we'd decided to wait and see how the competition went before confirming if we'd incorporate it here. But I couldn't help wondering if our heightened synchronization was because of the weight lifted off both of our shoulders.

There were no more gunmen stalking us. No more worries about the Devil's Dozen hassling Lou. Rafael was dealing with all that crap, and we could focus every bit of our energy on what mattered most to us: the skating.

Yesterday's short routine had gone as well as we could have hoped. For now, we were in fourth place, below two pairs whose greatest strength was their short program and the Russians who might be our greatest competition, just a single point ahead of us.

We both knew that our best time to shine was the free skate. Everything depended on what we did today.

I whirled around at one end of the rink and caught one of the other skaters staring at me for a second before he jerked his gaze away. The back of my neck prickled with the uneasy sensation of being watched.

He wasn't the first of our colleagues I'd spotted giving us skeptical looks, ranging from disapproving to unsettlingly curious. Of course our fellow skaters wouldn't have missed the scandal that'd nearly blown up our chances at Worlds before we'd set foot in Nagano's huge arena.

That was fine. I had nothing to be embarrassed about when it came to my personal relationships. With Lou, with the other men in her life, and with the other man in mine. My gaze darted across the rink, and I shared a quick smile with Niko.

My professional life, well… I did my best to ignore the

niggling voice in the back of my head that pointed out every hint of a wobble or twinge in my muscles. But it was impossible to forget that the last time I'd competed at Worlds, I'd totally fucked it up.

People watching me would be remembering that incident too. They'd be wondering whether I could actually pull off something decent this time without crashing and burning.

I was wondering that too. Every jump of my nerves was as much anxiety as excitement. I had a lot to prove here today.

But then, I also had way more support than I'd been able to count on back then. I had my gorgeous and incredibly talented partner skating alongside me. I had the fantastic coach who'd tracked me down halfway across the world ready to cheer me on. I even had my former rival sitting in the stands after giving us a quick pep talk this morning.

Things were definitely looking up. I'd built success on top of success in the past several months. That was all *I* needed to remember.

As I ran through the rest of my warm-up, I reminded myself of those facts over and over. When Lou glided over to me as the group warm-up time came to an end, I tugged her to me for a quick kiss.

She beamed back at me and sank down next to me on our bench. We leaned forward in matching stretches to finish warming up off the ice.

I was just raising my arms over my head when my phone's text alert tone pealed out. My pulse stuttered for a second before it sank in that none of our calls warning of danger had ever come to *my* phone. Maybe Quentin had decided to give a snarky tip or two before we went on.

I pulled my phone out of my equipment bag and tapped the screen to see the message.

In the first second, I just stared at the name at the top of the text. *Mom.* I hadn't talked to her in ages—hadn't wanted to exacerbate her already shaky relationship with Dad by reminding him of the career she'd supported and he'd never approved of. We'd exchanged occasional texts while I was staying at my grandparents' place, but not since I'd started training again with Niko.

She might be following the competitive circuit on the down low. I glanced to the actual message, expecting it to be words of encouragement and good luck that would feel bittersweet no matter how much I knew she meant them.

Hey, honey. I know it's been a while, but that's my fault. And it's been too long. I realize I can't make up for all that lost time, but I still wanted to be here for you and show how much I believe in you!

I blinked, struggling to process what she meant. "Be here for me"? It almost sounded like—

With another ping, a new text appeared. *I can see you right now. Look across the arena, about ten rows up.*

My jaw dropped. She was literally *here*? In Japan? She'd come all the way from the US to watch me compete?

How had she explained that trip to Dad?

My head jerked up. I scanned the stands on the opposite side of the arena—and spotted a familiar slim figure with auburn hair like mine, waving eagerly several rows above rink-level.

As I raised my hand to return the gesture in a daze, my

attention slid to the figure sitting next to her, and my arm froze in mid-air.

Dad was here too. Sitting beside her, looking a little stiff from what I could judge at that distance, his expression tight. But he lifted his hand in a brief wave as well, giving me a particle of acknowledgment.

Holy hell. How in the world had this happened?

I lowered my phone to my lap and realized Lou was peering at me. "What's wrong? What were the messages about?"

"Nothing—nothing you need to worry about," I said quickly, knowing she must be even more sensitive to unexpected news than I was. "My parents are here. They came to watch."

Lou's eyebrows leapt up. "Parents, plural? Your mom *and* dad? I thought your dad hated skating."

I swallowed hard. "He does. At least, he has my entire life, up until the last time I spoke to him a couple of years ago."

If my nerves had been jittering before, now they were doing jumping jacks all through my gut. As much as I appreciated Mom's gesture, even if I didn't totally understand what it meant, I kind of wished she hadn't told me until after our routine.

What if I screwed up in front of them? In front of Dad? That'd just be proving him right, wouldn't it? He'd feel justified in assuming my skating had always been a waste of time.

Lou squeezed my forearm. "Hey. Don't let it get to you. We'll still go out there and skate our best. What he thinks didn't matter before and it doesn't matter now."

I dragged in a breath, trying to absorb her certainty. Fighting against the sensation of Dad's judgment pressing down on me.

He was probably sneering mentally right now as he took in my shimmery costume and—

A hand clapped firmly against my shoulder from behind. I flinched and jerked around to see a middle-aged man I didn't recognize.

He made a gesture of apology. "Didn't mean to startle you, Jasper. I'm Jim Gunner with Skate Canada. Mostly I push paper, so we haven't gotten a chance to talk before."

Skate Canada was the official figure skating organization in my family's home country. I scrambled to set my thoughts in order. "Oh. Hi! Good to meet you."

Gunner laughed in a deep rumble that reminded me of dynamite. "No need to worry. I'm here to give my compliments. I wanted to tell you and your partner how much I enjoyed your trio skate with Quentin Wolf. It was beautiful work, especially considering that, from what I understand, you pulled it together very quickly."

His smile shone on both me and Lou. Lou grinned in response, and I found myself doing the same. "Thank you. I'm so glad it made an impact."

"Oh, it did that. I expect there'll be talk about this year's Worlds and your part in it for years to come. You've already left your mark no matter how you do today. If either of you ever decide you'd like to switch over to the Great White North, give us a call, you hear? That goes for Mr. Wolfe too!"

His praise washed over me, the warmth of his comments sweeping away the panic that'd gripped me moments before. "Thank you," I said again, more emphatically. "That means a lot to me."

"We'll give it some thought," Lou piped up, her grin widening. "And I hope you enjoy our routine today just as much."

Gunner caught Niko's eyes. "As much as I appreciate what you're doing with your coaching, I hope I see you on the competitive circuit again someday soon too, Mr. Okabe. Now I'd better get to my seat!"

With that, he shuffled off. Lou watched him go and shook her head with a light chuckle. "He's quite the character."

"Yeah," I said, my mind still reeling—but in a good way this time.

Maybe my career hadn't gone quite the way I'd imagined, but I'd still come so far from my early days learning the basic jumps and spins. I'd won medals; I'd gained enough fans to earn a playful nickname. There was no world in which that made me a failure.

I got to decide what success meant to me. My dad didn't get any say in it. Even if today was an epic flop, I'd still know I'd made it. I had so many chances to do even more ahead of me.

I'd climbed dozens of mountains to get this far. I'd struggled and fought and pushed with all my might to claw my way to this spot. Was I really going to let my asshole father pull me down now?

No way in hell.

With a renewed surge of confidence, I nudged Lou's shoulder. "You know what? Who cares what the other pairs do? I say we go for the new transition either way."

Lou's eyes widened. "Are you sure? We're not exactly solid with it yet. You seemed pretty iffy about incorporating it at the last practice."

"I know, I know. But listen. If we can pull it off, then that's it—we're almost guaranteed a medal, if not the gold. And if we fumble it… Isn't it better to fail at something incredible than to have our routine be flawless but uninspiring? If it doesn't happen this time, then we have another whole year to practice." My lips pulled into another grin. "So what do you say? You want to give it a shot, Punk?"

Lou laughed and took my hand, squeezing it hard. "More than anything in the world."

And just like that, it was all okay. No matter what happened now, I knew we were going to survive it. Whether Dad watched me fly or watched me fall, I wouldn't be shaken by him.

Not now, and not ever again.

TWENTY-SEVEN

Luciana

I THOUGHT I'd put on a good face with Jasper, but I'd be lying if I said I wasn't nervous.

As I watched the many pairs before us take to the ice, my heart pounded a million miles a minute. Why had we ended up toward the end of the line-up? All this waiting was killing me.

Of course, it might have been even worse skating early and then waiting over and over to see if our current rank would be displaced by someone else.

My foot tapped against the floor with clicks of my skate guard until I noticed and held it still. The pair who'd just launched into their routine were right before us—we were up next. I needed to find my inner calm and stay focused.

The truth was that despite my anxiety, my childhood

self was doing somersaults in my chest. No matter what score we earned, just being here at Worlds was a longtime dream I'd barely allowed myself to consider might be possible.

I just had to keep reaching for the gold with each competition season, and someday I might be known among the greats. Skating here in Nagano was just one step along a much larger—and incredibly thrilling —journey.

My gaze followed the pair on the ice. They launched into an impressive lift that had me holding my breath, but the woman had to drop her raised foot too quickly on the dismount to recover her balance.

I couldn't criticize her. It was totally possible we'd have a much more epic wipeout when we attempted our spin to lift transition.

No, don't think about that. We had nailed it a couple of times. I knew it was possible.

All we had to do was repeat what we'd already done. When I thought about it that way, it only sounded slightly terrifying.

I glanced toward the stands. Niko, standing behind me and Jasper, caught my gaze with a typical sunny smile. He exuded nothing but warm confidence.

I found myself grinning back at him. Then my attention slid farther, to where Rafael and Quentin were sitting next to each other in seats a few rows up. They both nodded to me when they saw me looking their way, Rafael offering one of his subdued smiles that meant as much as a broad grin and Quentin offering a thumbs up.

A couple rows higher, Emi waved eagerly at me. She

was beaming so bright you'd have thought she'd already won a gold medal.

As I drew my gaze away, it snagged on a face I hadn't expected to see. Beckett was sitting in the crowd, watching the current skaters intently with his hand at his chin.

My heart skipped a beat in surprise, and I scanned the rest of the seats more carefully. In a matter of seconds, I picked out not just the Blood Hunter but also the two older men who'd arrived for my confrontation with Mom —the ones who'd hesitated the longest before accepting Rafael as my replacement.

When they caught me staring, one gave a brief nod. The other kept up an impenetrably stern expression.

A fresh jitter ran through my nerves. Beckett and the Blood Hunter had been my allies for a while—I could believe they were only here out of personal interest. But the other two…

Had they come to evaluate how serious I really was about my skating? To find proof that I really was giving up the Devil's Dozen life with this other career?

I took a deep breath. Let them watch. I knew how committed I was. They couldn't help but see that I was on the same level as the other skaters here—a level I couldn't have reached if I wasn't practicing like my life depended on it.

At least they'd believed in me enough to think it was possible I had a valid alternative. Mom had never bothered to do that much.

I was so far in my head that I barely noticed the end of the previous pair's routine. Seeing them heading toward the boards, I pushed to my feet with a rush of giddy exhilaration. Jasper and I stepped out onto the ice, knowing exactly what words we'd hear next.

"Our next skaters are representing the United States: Luna Garcia and Jasper St. Pierre."

Jasper and I pushed off across the ice. We glided in a loop around the edge of the arena, giving our muscles a slight additional warm-up and the audience a chance to take in our costumes.

My gaze sought out my other men again. Emi let out a whoop from her seat. A smile touched my lips as the sensation swept through me that they were all here with me on the ice almost as solidly as my partner, who was squeezing my hand.

We struck our opening pose. The rink had gone quiet, so still I'd swear the judges would hear my heart thudding away. But there was nothing left in it but joy and determination now. I was going to show everyone what I was put on this earth to do.

The first notes of our song resonated through the air, and I felt the music right down to my bones. I'd skated to this melody so often it might as well have been a part of me, like the rhythm of my breath and my pulse.

The two of us became parallel shooting stars as we shot across the rink. I kept my face relaxed, my expression languid. My brows flicked up only slightly as my partner lifted me up into our complex opening lift. One beat, two beats, a third—whirling across the ice with the lilting notes.

After Jasper lowered me, we took off again in a darting game of cat and mouse that went along perfectly with the swelling cadence that pumped through the PA speakers.

We jumped high, spun fast, flowing from one move into the next like our bodies had been made for nothing else.

The entire time, the exhilaration that'd filled me buoyed me up. I'd won my way to freedom. I'd faced the world I'd come from, conquered it, and set off into new territory I was making my own. Now I was going to conquer this challenge too—and have a lot more fun doing it.

And I'd made it here with four amazing men who were still supporting me through every leap across the ice.

We whipped around, and Jasper grasped my hand to propel me into the spin that would lead into our next lift. My pulse hiccupped just once, and then I latched on to the peace in his gray-green eyes. The storm clouds so often there had faded away.

He was as immersed in the emotions of the routine as I was.

I leaned into his hold, letting him swing me across the ice. A chilly wind whipped up as I sped around just inches above the frozen surface.

A touch of cold slipped right into my chest. What if we screwed this up? What if it all came crashing down in the next few seconds?

Wait—why was I even thinking that?

Jasper's hand was perfectly solid and steady in mine. Jasper had always been there to lift me and catch me when I needed him to.

Maybe I'd still been holding back just a tiny bit, afraid of letting go completely and trusting him to hold my very life in his hands. But when I considered that thought, I could see how ridiculous it was.

I loved him, and I believed in him too. We could pull this off together. I wasn't alone, and there was no one left in my life who wanted to tie me down.

That last shred of doubt fled my body. Jasper yanked me up, and I soared into his arms like the angel Niko had dubbed me. A shared gasp warbled over the music as Jasper flung me up over his head straight out of the spin.

I could really fly without my mother's threats bearing down on me. I could launch myself far beyond the cruel world she'd tried to trap me in.

As my foot touched down again, I tensed my calf just before a wobble could creep through it. Then we were gliding across the ice again in perfect synchronization.

We'd done it. Maybe a hair away from a fault, but we'd fulfilled every requirement for full marks.

A laugh of pure delight tumbled from Jasper's lips, and I couldn't help echoing it. We swept through the rest of the routine on a rush of pure elation.

Then, hands clasped together, we lifted them high in our ending pose, my body arced against his. The song finished. Silence reigned.

And applause exploded through the arena.

As we skated over to the stands while the next pair took to the ice, I caught Emi chanting our names. More whoops carried out from across the audience. I sank down onto the bench where we'd receive our scores, trembling from the exertion of the routine and my own awed satisfaction.

Jasper slung his arm around my shoulders. "We really fucking did that, Punk."

I let out another laugh. "We sure did. You know, I feel like I've won something whether we get a medal or not."

"We'd better get *something*," Jasper muttered under his breath, but he hadn't stopped smiling.

The English announcer lifted his voice to declare our scores. "Luna Garcia and Jasper St. Pierre have earned in the free skate one hundred and fifty-three point two five."

My jaw dropped. I couldn't find the will to reel it back in. We'd gotten more than a hundred and fifty points— that had to be close to the record.

Niko cheered and grabbed us in a joint hug. "That's your best score yet. They saw just how fantastic you were —and how much you risked with the difficulty of those moves."

I gripped his arm, my mind whirling. "That—that puts us in first place, doesn't it?"

"You bet!"

"The Russians still have to go," Jasper reminded me as we moved to our spot in the stands. "They're up last."

I took in the grin that stretched from ear to ear across his face and elbowed him. "And you look so worried about it."

"Hey, I'll take a silver. I'm still having trouble wrapping my head around that score—and that we pulled the whole thing off so well here at Worlds. Holy crap—my *dad* saw that."

I hugged him close. Hopefully his dad would start to realize that Jasper's talent wasn't something that should be suppressed, but even if he didn't, it wouldn't mean a thing about the man beside me.

We watched the last few pairs compete, but the whole

time I felt weirdly detached. I could appreciate the artistry of the movements, but the adrenaline rush had left me in a giddy state that gave the whole experience an unreal quality. Maybe I was actually dreaming?

Then the Russian pair glided onto the rink, and reality came back into sharper focus. I took in the woman's immaculate bun and their complimentary costumes, not a seam out of place. A lump rose in my throat.

Music drifted down from the speakers, and the pair became a pair of twin bullets, shooting across the length of the arena. The song they chose to accompany their routine was full of energy, a rock song that felt charged with electricity. The drumbeat matched their quick footwork; not once did the pair fall out of rhythm.

"Their quad throw should be coming up," Niko murmured at my side. "Any second now…"

And then there it was. The man lifted his partner high into the air, and she was airborne. She spun in four tight rotations. Her form was excellent, her landing beyond beautiful.

I could admit it was impressive to see. I stayed braced in my seat through the rest of the routine, admiring their poise and athleticism. I didn't see a single stumble.

When they hit their final pose, I sagged backward with a whoosh of a sigh. "Wow. They *are* good."

Niko clicked his tongue. "You two were very good too."

"I guess it comes down to what the judges think of it. The overall difficulty across all the moves is about the same, right?"

Our coach nodded. "No surprises."

"I have no idea how this will go," Jasper said. "They were stunning."

Niko raised his eyebrows at us. "I think yours had more heart."

I resisted the urge to squirm as we waited for the scores to be announced.

The announcer's voice crackled through the speakers. "Oleg Baranov and Yana Andreyeva have earned in the free skate a score of one hundred and fifty-one point five three."

My brain stumbled in its attempt to do math with the pressure of anticipation clouding my thoughts. All around us, people were clapping and leaning over to pat my and Jasper's shoulders. Shouts of congratulations rained down on us.

"You won!" Niko crowed. "You two got the gold. I knew you could!"

A choked laugh broke from my lips, and tears that were all happiness sprang to my eyes. I clutched Jasper and then Niko in the tightest of hugs. "Díos mio. Oh my God. We really did it."

Niko's phone started buzzing. He let out a laugh of his own. "There are all the reporters wanting interviews. And maybe some new sponsors too."

"Oh my God," I said again. My mind was spinning too fast for me to form any other words.

I blinked away my tears and smiled toward the stands where my other two men and my first real friend were watching. This victory was for all of us.

And maybe not just the people I knew of. I had to hope that everyone in the Devil's Dozen had been watching this competition, whether in person or on the TV. That they'd seen just how far my other interests had taken me.

If there were other heirs out there who weren't sure that the path most directly in front of them was the one that was actually right, then I'd just shown them there was another way. They could be who they wanted and still triumph.

TWENTY-EIGHT

Six months later

Luciana

I LEANED against the boards around the rink next to Jasper while our new coach rubbed his hands together, like he always did when he had something important to say. Niko had recommended Jerry Valdez to us, having worked with him for several months when Jerry was on an extended visit to Japan.

"Let me know what you two really think," he said in his gruff but warm tone that reminded me in a bittersweet way of Coach Balakin. "But I figure that since you two can pull off that tricky transition smooth as butter now, it's time to up the ante a little more. What if we added a throw at the end of the lift?"

My heart beat a little faster, considering how that would work. "It could be pretty fantastic. But we've only been really solid with the transition for the last few weeks."

Jasper cocked his head at me. "Could be worth a try, though, don't you think?"

I wet my lips and grinned. "Let's give the new routine one more run-through, and I'll imagine it to see how it feels in the moment."

Jerry swept his arm toward the ice. "Have at it."

We waved to Quentin, who'd also come under Jerry's wing and was practicing his singles routines alternating with Jasper and me. He gave us a thumbs up and a cocky smile before gliding out of the way.

It'd taken a while to hone our new routine for the next competitive circuit. We could skip the qualifying rounds because of our success last year, but we still needed to compete at Nationals in a few months. That should be plenty of time to make one more adjustment, though.

Jerry started the song, a bass heavy but still melodic pop song that had appealed to both me and Jasper, and my partner and I launched into the opening moves. We soared across the ice, every movement in harmony.

I'd done this hundreds of times now, but my heart still lifted when we jumped and spun together.

My nerves no longer jittered when we swept from the death spiral into our now-trademark lift. As Jasper whirled me around, I pictured what it would feel like for him to fling me into the air rather than lowering me like he usually did.

When we reached the end of the routine, my tee was damp with sweat. We'd been at this for hours already.

As we skated back to Jerry, I clapped my hands. "I think we could pull it off. Let's give it a shot!"

Jasper squeezed my shoulder. "I'm on board."

Jerry set his hands on his hips. "Perfect. I'll tinker with the moves afterward to smooth everything out, and we can get started tomorrow. Now, Lou, you could still lift your skates a little higher in that one footwork sequence. And Jasper, I think you could get more air with your triple Axel."

"Don't forget to remind them about their hand positioning in the first lift!"

At the cheerful voice, I glanced around Jerry and realized Niko had come back from his water break. He beamed at us while he shucked off his skate guards.

As Niko stepped onto the ice, Jasper wagged a finger at him teasingly. "You need to take off the coaching cap and focus on your own routine."

"That's right, old man," Quentin called out from the other end of the rink. "You've got a lot of work to do if you want to beat me once we get to Worlds."

Niko had decided to take a step back from coaching for a while and return to competing himself, joining us under Jerry's guidance. But he couldn't stop himself from weighing in here and there.

Thankfully, he also didn't take it hard when we chided him about it. He chuckled and tugged Jasper to him for a quick kiss.

"I can do that," he said, and blew a kiss to me as well before skating off.

Jerry simply shook his head in amusement. "All right, let's see you each go through your current routine one more time, and I'll give you a few more notes to run through in your dreams tonight."

By the time we were heading out the door, a pleasant burn had spread through all my muscles. I stretched my arms over my head and let out a glorious sigh. "This is the life."

"It is a pretty awesome one," Jasper agreed, and caught my hand to hold it.

Quentin came up by my side and took my other hand, not to be outdone. "I've got no complaints."

"As long as Emi keeps sending me those cases of Calpis, I'm right at home," Niko put in, making us all laugh.

We ambled down the Boston street that *was* feeling more and more like home with every passing week. I loved the noise and activity of a big city, and despite the Harvester's intervention, this had been my favorite of the places we'd stayed during our travels for training and competitions.

The guys had easily agreed to settling down here for the time being. Quentin had no interest in returning to his hometown where his mother would be more than happy to harass him, and we were close enough to Ontario that it wasn't difficult for Jasper to head up north to visit his family from time to time.

Right after Worlds, his mom had asked his dad for a divorce and moved back to Canada. Apparently bringing him to the championships had been her last-ditch effort to fix their relationship after she'd realized she couldn't tolerate his awful treatment of their son any longer. Mr. St. Pierre hadn't reformed enough, so she'd kicked him to the curb—like I happened to think she really should have done at least a decade ago.

But it was good to see how happy Jasper looked when I joined him on one of his trips across the border.

The loft we'd scored was just a few blocks from the arena where we were training. About halfway there, my phone chimed with an incoming text. I hefted my equipment back farther over my shoulder and pulled out the phone.

Emi had sent one of her emoji-filled messages. *Just booked my plane tickets for next month! Can't wait to see all of you!! You'd better be ready to go out on the town and have fun!*

My lips jumped into a smile as I typed my response. *I'm always ready. Just a few more weeks!*

A chance to hang out with my best friend was just what I needed. And Niko always brightened up even more than his usual cheery self when his sister was around.

As I slid my phone back into my pocket, Jasper gave me a subtle nudge. "There's another pair of them."

His tone was wry. I glanced up and noted the two brawny men in sports jackets sitting in a car across the street from our loft building. It took all my effort not to roll my eyes as a mix of irritation and amusement swept through me.

"Always keeping an eye on us," I said, matching Jasper's tone. "I wonder how long it'll take before Rafael's sure we're okay."

Quentin raised an eyebrow at me. "*You're* okay, you

mean. We don't kid ourselves that it's the rest of us he's so concerned about protecting."

I elbowed him playfully. "Aw, he likes all of you too."

Niko looked as if he was suppressing the urge to wave at our supposedly low-key guards. "How's his alliance with the Harvester working out?"

I grabbed my keys to unlock the building's door. "Pretty well, from what he's told me. I guess that the business they went in on together has been really profitable. I'm sure he'll have lots to tell us about that tonight."

My heart lifted at the thought of Rafael's visit. In his role as the new Deadly Rose, he needed to spend a fair bit of time in Austin in the old Cordova mansion, keeping the main underlings in line. But after he'd gotten everything under control to begin with, he'd picked out some key people who could run things well when he wasn't there. Now he usually stayed with us for at least a couple of days every week.

But I always looked forward to those visits. As much as I understood why he couldn't be here every day like my other men, I treasured every minute I could get.

Once things were more settled for all of us, we'd find a way to be together all the time.

Rafael had made an alliance with the Harvester shortly after he'd taken over the Deadly Rose title, and part of their deal was that the Harvester's people in Boston kept a lookout to make sure no one threatened us. But so far the rest of the Devil's Dozen had left me completely alone since the World Championships, thank God.

The elevator let us out right outside the door to our

two-story unit. With as many as five of us sharing the space at any given time, and some of them men with very strong opinions, we'd figured it was best to leave lots of room for people to spread out. We all had our own small bedrooms on the second floor, and the first floor was divided by the furnishings into several distinct areas with a different focus.

I was just raising the key to the lock when the door swung open on its own. A massive figure grinned down at me.

I dropped my bag and flung my arms around my former bodyguard. "Rafael! You got in early. I didn't think you'd be here until later tonight."

Rafael hugged me back tightly and then eased back to enjoy a lingering kiss. "I've been here for about an hour—and I made Cuban sandwiches for everyone. I figured all that work on the ice has probably left you awfully hungry."

Quentin's eyes gleamed eagerly. "You know it. Where's the grub?"

Rafael laughed and motioned us all into the loft. I made a beeline for the table, which he'd already set out with a sandwich at five of the six chairs. "Is everything okay in Austin?" I asked over my shoulder. "How's *your* work going?"

Rafael sank down next to me. "I've sorted out some things that needed sorting—faster than I thought I'd be able to. But you handed the job over to me because you didn't want to be bothered with all the details, right?"

I wrinkled my nose at him, but he had a point. "Fine. But if there's ever anything you *want* to talk about, you know you can. We all have a lot more experience with that part of my old life than I wish we did."

Rafael offered me a softer smile and gave my ponytail an affectionate hug. "And I'd like to make sure you never have to experience any more of it. Don't worry—I'm enjoying the challenge. And I'm happy with how the changes I've made are panning out. What about all of you? Anything new on the skating side?"

An answering smile sprang to my face. "We've really hit our stride with our new free skate routine. So much that Coach Valdez wants us to increase the difficulty."

His eyebrows rose. "Again? I thought you were already pulling off some kind of miracle."

Quentin smirked. "They do call this guy Saint Jasper for a reason, I guess…"

I got the impression that Jasper kicked his one-time rival—lightly—under the table. He turned to Rafael. "In the skating world, you always have to be looking for ways to stretch your abilities even farther. Because everyone else always is too, so otherwise you get left behind."

The corners of Rafael's mouth curled with amusement. "Sounds a lot like the criminal world, actually."

"Their routine is going to be jaw-dropping with the new addition," Niko declared around a big bite of his Cuban sandwich. "It'll be fantastic if we can all make it to Prague next year."

I glanced at him, knitting my brow. "Prague?"

Niko grinned at me. "That's where the Winter Olympics are being held, remember?"

Electricity zinged through my veins. I hadn't let myself

think that far ahead. The idea of competing at the actual Olympics felt like a dream within a dream.

But it really was within our grasp, wasn't it? We'd won gold at Worlds. The Olympics would be a similar level of competition, even if it got a lot more fanfare.

Díos mio, the number of people who'd be watching if we performed there…

My heart fluttered with excitement, and I caught a matching gleam in both Jasper's and Quentin's eyes.

"Yeah, that'd be amazing, all right," Jasper said.

I thumped my fist on the table. "Then we'll just have to make it happen."

Rafael hummed to himself. "It sounds like I'm going to have to check out my new empire's European holdings so I can find plenty of excuses to be over on that side of the ocean by then."

I nudged him under the table. "You're the boss. You can make up excuses."

He laughed. "Good point. Now, come on, everyone. Dig into those sandwiches, or I'm going to think you don't like my cooking."

Quentin immediately stuffed the end of the sandwich into his mouth, carby bread and all. "You are never allowed to stop cooking for us," he insisted after he swallowed. "You can have all my cheat days."

Jasper shot the other guy an amused glance. "What does that mean—you won't eat any carbs at all the rest of the week?"

"Hey, I make it work."

"It's fine," Niko said serenely. "Anything he doesn't eat, I definitely will."

I leaned back in my chair amid the companionable warmth of their banter and couldn't hold back the smile that stretched across my lips.

This was a real home. This was exactly where I wanted to be. As hard as it still was to believe, everything in my life had clicked into place.

After all my clawing toward freedom to escape Mom and her influence, I'd been able to stop fighting and pursue the life I'd wanted. I could fill my days with different kinds of power—the kinds that came from agility and beauty rather than brutality.

I was in charge of my own destiny now. And with the four men I loved by my side, I knew I was finally on the right path, heading toward a future full of joy.

ABOUT THE AUTHORS

Eva Chance is a pen name for contemporary romance written by Amazon top 100 bestselling author Eva Chase. If you love gritty romance, dominant men, and fierce women who never have to choose, look no further.

Eva lives in Canada with her family. She loves stories both swoony and supernatural, and strong women and the men who appreciate them.

Connect with Eva online:
www.evachase.com
eva@evachase.com

Harlow King is a long-time fan of all things dark, edgy, and steamy. She can't wait to share her contemporary reverse harem stories.